BEYOND THE FURY

Ruth & Rich,
 Enjoy the book!
 Cassandra Loker

BEYOND THE FURY

Cassandra Lokker

Copyright © 2007 by Cassandra Lokker

All rights reserved. No part of this book shall be reproduced or transmitted in any form or by any means, electronic, mechanical, magnetic, photographic including photocopying, recording or by any information storage and retrieval system, without prior written permission of the publisher. No patent liability is assumed with respect to the use of the information contained herein. Although every precaution has been taken in the preparation of this book, the publisher and author assume no responsibility for errors or omissions. Neither is any liability assumed for damages resulting from the use of the information contained herein.

This is a work of fiction. Names, characters, places, and incidents either are the product of the author's imagination or are used fictitiously. Any resemblance to actual events or locales or persons, living or dead, is entirely coincidental.

ISBN 0-7414-4134-9

Cover art: Kirbee Tagney, Carrie Lokker

Published by:
INFI∞ITY
PUBLISHING.COM
1094 New DeHaven Street, Suite 100
West Conshohocken, PA 19428-2713
Info@buybooksontheweb.com
www.buybooksontheweb.com
Toll-free (877) BUY BOOK
Local Phone (610) 941-9999
Fax (610) 941-9959

Printed in the United States of America
Printed on Recycled Paper
Published July 2007

Acknowledgments

A great deal of time and effort has been expended in the writing of this novella. Several sources proved to be invaluable as I researched and prepared for writing. Such books and forms of research are included in the Author's Note. Without a historical base for the story, I wouldn't have had the necessary information in reference to the cyclone and the events that took place following that day.

In addition, I would like to thank the members of Fiction Writing/English 304 for their comments and encouragement during the writing of the short story that started me on the road to writing this novella. I would also like to thank my advisor and professor, James Schaap, for overseeing this project and offering the support and knowledge regarding the process of writing fiction.

My friends and family have been a tremendous help throughout this project as well. I am especially indebted to my friend and helpful editor, Ashley Knegendorf, who read early drafts of the manuscript and offered up detailed critiques and editing suggestions. I would also like to thank my friends Karyn Zuidhof, Heidi Beukelman, Sara Top, Ruth Lynch, and Michelle Vis for their comments and valuable editing skills during the composition of the short story. I also thank Karyn, Heidi, and my sister Carrie Lokker for their help in researching character names for the particular period in history. My mother also deserves heartfelt thanks, for without her initial idea, this book would have never been a reality. I also thank her for reading early drafts of the manuscript and making suggestions on how to improve the storyline. My dad has been a great encouragement to me as I completed this book as well. Thank you, Dad.

To everyone who assisted in this project in some way, I thank you. Your help has been greatly appreciated.

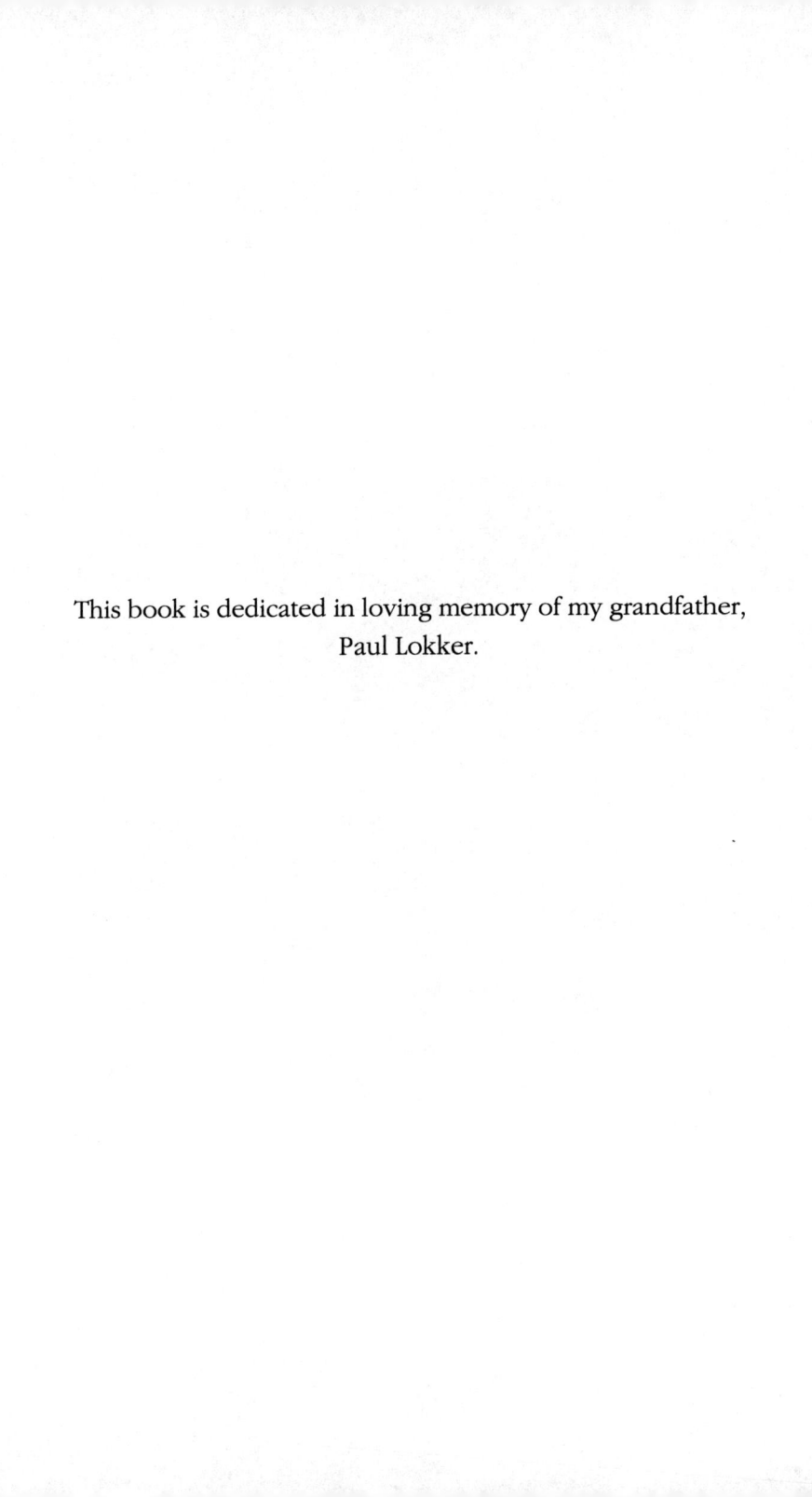

This book is dedicated in loving memory of my grandfather, Paul Lokker.

One

"All right, children," Caitlyn Schmidt said, clapping her hands to get everyone's attention. "Please sit down so we can get started. We have a lot to do today."

"Oral examinations," said Adam Lewis, a fifth year student. "Who wants to do that?"

"Now, Adam," Caitlyn admonished. "I don't want to hear any complaints from you. If you don't behave, you'll have to stand in the corner."

"Yes, Miss Schmidt," the boy responded.

"Well, let's take attendance. Anita Brown?"

"Present, Ma'am."

"Phillip Brown?"

"Present."

"Lizzy Carlson?"

Lizzy lifted her hand in acknowledgement, and was about to speak when the school door opened. A blast of cold, December air drifted into the room as a young girl hurried inside. She was clad in a heavy, wool coat, her long, brown hair partially covered by a knit hat that extended over her ears. Two little boys, presumably her brothers, shyly followed her and lingered in the doorway. The girl removed her hat, revealing thick ringlets that cascaded down her back.

"We're sorry to be late, Ma'am," she apologized. "Pa had to finish with the chores."

Caitlyn smiled at the girl as she approached the three newcomers. "That's fine, but please do not make a habit of being late in the future."

"Oh, we won't, Ma'am. I promise."

"I am Miss Schmidt," Caitlyn said to the girl. "What are your names?" She gestured toward the children, urging them to come further into the room.

"I'm Elaina Torgeson," the girl replied as she removed her mittens. "And these are my brothers Joseph and Anthony. Our family just moved here in the fall. Ma and Pa thought it was time my brothers and I came to school."

"Well, we're glad you have come to join us, aren't we, children?" Caitlyn said with a smile, turning to the class. "Now, boys and girls, let's be sure to make the Torgesons feel welcome."

Caitlyn turned back to the children now clustered near the front of the classroom. Elaina appeared the most confident of the three. She held the hand of her youngest brother as if to give him reassurance that everything was all right. Joseph, the second oldest, looked around the room with interest as if to assess the other students. Perhaps he was looking for friends already. Caitlyn wanted to make the newcomers feel at ease, so she immediately did her best to draw the children into the day's activities.

"You may put your coats in the cloakroom and then join us," she said. "During recess you will have to stay inside so we can talk about your schoolwork. Today we are having oral examinations, which of course you will be unable to do. You will have to begin your school work after the Christmas break."

Elaina nodded. She then led her brothers to the cloakroom, and Caitlyn resumed taking attendance.

At morning recess, Caitlyn gathered the Torgeson children around her desk. The three children had seemed to fit in well with the other students, and it looked as if their transition to a new school environment would be quite smooth. But now there was the matter of the children's education. She must know their grade level before she could assign them to a class. And like all of her students, she was eager to discover who these children were. Where did they live? Who were their parents? Why had they come to New Richmond? And there were even questions of general curiosity. What did the children like to do outside of school? Was Elaina the kind of girl that would help her mother with the daily chores? Did she enjoy playing outdoors, or was she more interested in reading, sewing, or other such things? And what about the boys? She knew from experience that boys were unpredictable by nature. It would only be a matter of time before she would find out.

"Am I right in assuming you have attended school elsewhere?" Caitlyn asked, laying aside her thoughts and directing her question at Elaina.

"Yes, at home in South Dakota. Here are our school records. Ma thought you might want to see them. If you have any questions, Pa said he could come by for a few minutes before school tomorrow."

"Thank you," Caitlyn replied as she reached for the documents. She scanned them quickly, noting the children's ages and level of education. It appeared that Elaina was a very bright student, earning high marks in almost all of her classes. She had already reached the seventh grade level with recommendation that she be admitted to eighth. Joseph, age ten and Anthony, age seven were stated as being in the fourth and second grade classes respectively. Both boys had achieved good marks in many of their classes, and in Caitlyn's eyes, they had reached an acceptable level for their ages.

"I can see that you're all very good students," Caitlyn said as she looked up at the children. She directed a smile toward each child, hoping to make them all feel more at ease. The boys in particular looked as if they were somewhat uncomfortable. "As I said earlier, you can begin your studies in the spring term, but until then, I can give you your readers. You can take them home and study them over break so you will be ready when school begins again. Judging by these records here, I'd say that you'd be caught up with the rest of the students in no time. For the rest of the day, you are welcome to stay and observe the examinations. Perhaps the other students will be able to teach you a great deal from what they have learned this term."

Elaina nodded, glancing at her brothers.

"Oh, and tonight, there's a school social. You are welcome to come and bring your family. I'd really like to meet your ma and pa. It's sure to be a fun time."

"We'll have to ask Ma and Pa," Joseph said. "They're awfully busy."

"When did you say your family came to New Richmond?" Caitlyn asked.

"Just a few months ago," Elaina replied. "Pa wanted to get settled before winter set in, so there was a lot to do. That's why we didn't come to school at the beginning of the term. But Ma wouldn't hear of us missing any more school."

"Well, I'm sure I'm not the first, but let me welcome you to New Richmond. I hope your family likes it here."

"Oh, we do," Elaina responded, her dark eyes gleaming with excitement. "It's so beautiful here… the hills, the trees… It's nothing like South Dakota. And the people are so nice."

"Well, I'm glad you like the area. I also hope you will like it here at school," she said. "But now, why don't you children take your seats. It's time to ring the bell. Recess is over."

"Miss Schmidt, can I ring the bell?" little Anthony asked. "Please."

Caitlyn smiled and led him to the door. "Sure, Anthony, but just this once."

Anthony beamed and hurried ahead of her.

After all of the children had completed their exams that afternoon, Caitlyn greeted the proud parents of her students. Many had come to see their child's work and hear their oral presentations. Caitlyn encouraged everyone to return to the school that evening for the social, and after they all had gone, she turned to the empty rows of desks with a sigh. How wonderful this term had been with so much learned and achieved. And tonight they would celebrate. The students certainly deserved it. She was looking forward to an evening spent with family and friends, good food, and fellowship. It had been so long since there had been a social gathering of this nature. Winter had already set in with a brutal chill, and no one wanted to travel great distances on cold nights. But tonight was an exception. The Christmas season was a time for celebration, and Caitlyn couldn't wait to gather with the others. But first, she must get home. She had her dinner to prepare for the social, and she wanted it to be perfect.

Two

Caitlyn arrived at the schoolhouse a few hours later with her parents, all three eager to escape the bitterly cold wind. They hurried inside, Mr. Schmidt helping his wife and daughter out of their heavy coats. Caitlyn looked around the bustling room, hoping to see her brother-in-law Matthew and her sister Rena. The couple had planned to bring their daughter Madeline to the social, as she would most likely begin school in the next few years. Not seeing them, she turned to her parents.

"Did Matthew and Rena say anything about whether or not they were coming?" Caitlyn asked.

"Yes, I think Rena mentioned it," her mother replied. She glanced toward the door, craning her neck to see around the people clustered near the doorway. "Oh, wait, I think I see them now. And doesn't little Maddie look just darling in that new winter coat of hers. Let's go say hello."

The three moved toward the door, inching their way toward their relatives.

"Auntie Caitlyn!" three-year-old Madeline cried in excitement. "Auntie Caitlyn."

"You came," Caitlyn said as she scooped the girl into her arms.

"Of course," Rena responded. "You've been trying to convince us to come to one of these socials for quite a while now. So we finally came."

"Besides, who wouldn't want to celebrate the end of the term with the best teacher New Richmond has ever had?"

"Andrew!" Caitlyn exclaimed as Matthew's brother stepped out of the cloakroom. "What are you doing here?"

"I thought I'd spend the evening out for a change. It sure is better than staying at the boardinghouse by myself all night." He extended his hand to her as if in greeting, and she placed her hand in his. "Now, Miss Schmidt, you must promise me a dance tonight. I wanted to be sure to make my request before others stepped in."

Caitlyn could feel her face growing warm, and she hated the thought that he could see how uncomfortable she was with this particular matter. "I don't think you'll have to worry about that, Mr. Foster," she said, replying with his earlier formal flair. "I don't see anyone here who would want to dance with me."

"We'll see about that," Andrew responded.

"Andrew Foster, you are impossible," she said, refusing the urge to stamp her foot and walk away.

"So Caitlyn, are you in charge of tonight's festivities?" Matthew asked, putting an end to the preceding conversation.

Caitlyn shook her head. "No, Gerald Hughes from the school board said he would get everything started. It should be any time now."

As if on cue, Mr. Hughes raised his voice over the clamorous crowd. "Before we eat," he announced in his booming voice, "I would like to thank our fine educator, Miss Schmidt, for seeing to our children's schooling over the past term. I would also like to congratulate the students on their hard work and dedication to their studies."

Applause swelled in the room, and Caitlyn knew she must be beaming with pride. She was so proud of her students and was eager to continue where they had left off when school resumed after Christmas break.

"Now, let's eat. I'm sure the women have prepared a feast for all of us."

Again there was applause, and a line quickly formed where the food had been placed near the front of the classroom. Caitlyn saw a few of her students across the room and began making her way toward them.

"Aren't you going to join us for supper?" her father asked.

"I'll be just a minute, Pa," she said, glancing over her shoulder. "You may go ahead and get your supper, and I'll find you later."

"All right, if you're sure."

Caitlyn nodded and turned back toward the students she had been seeking. But she didn't make it to her destination.

Elaina Torgeson, one of the new students, motioned to her. She stood against the back wall of the classroom, surrounded by what appeared to be her family.

"Elaina," Caitlyn said, drawing close. "I'm so glad you came. This must be your family."

Elaina grinned and gestured toward her brothers. "You already know Joseph and Anthony," she said. "And this is my ma and pa."

"Pleased to meet you, Miss Schmidt," Elaina's father said, extending his hand toward her. She noted the man's firm grasp as they shook hands. "I'm Henry Torgeson and this is my wife Hannah."

"It's wonderful to meet you," the woman said with a smile as she cradled a young child in her arms.

"Yes, I'm pleased to meet you too," Caitlyn responded. "And who is this?" She reached out a hand to gently stroke the baby's dark head.

"This is David," his mother said with a proud smile. "He'll be seven months next week."

"My, you certainly have your hands full then," Caitlyn remarked. "I'm sure you are glad to get some of your children off to school."

"Oh, yes, today was one of the most peaceful days in a long time. The children said they really enjoyed school. Of course, they were probably happy that they didn't have to do any studying, but that will change as soon as Christmas is over. I will make sure they study hard, Miss Schmidt. It's been awhile since they have been in school."

"I'm sure they will do just fine," Caitlyn assured her. "Why don't you all get some supper? Perhaps I'll see you later in the evening."

She turned back toward her family who had waited for her after all, and they sat down together to eat. They enjoyed the fried chicken, potatoes, and chocolate cake, the varying dishes representative of several different recipes. Before they could finish, the music began, the sound of the fiddle inviting everyone to get up and dance. Couples sought each other out and soon, the desks were cleared from the center of the room, creating a large dance floor. Mr. and Mrs. Schmidt didn't waste any time standing around to talk. They joined the others on the dance floor, and not long after, Matthew and Rena did the same. Caitlyn sat with Madeline on her lap as the couples danced around them. Andrew stood close by, also looking on.

"I want to dance too," Madeline said, glancing up at Caitlyn, pleading etched in her dark blue eyes.

"Well, Maddie," Andrew said, kneeling down in front of the child. He lifted her from Caitlyn's arms and spun her in a circle. "I'll dance with you."

She giggled as Andrew lifted her high in the air, spinning them both in a circle. Caitlyn smiled at the child's obvious happiness. She knew Andrew and Madeline were very close. Rena often said that Andrew spoiled his niece to great proportions. There was nothing he wouldn't do for the child.

"Excuse me, Miss."

Caitlyn glanced up at the sound of the somewhat timid greeting. She found herself gazing into deep, brown eyes, eyes so dark, their depths seemed endless. His hair, not nearly as dark as his eyes, framed his head in light waves. She wouldn't have defined it as curly, but yet, there was a natural curl to the wisps that rested on his forehead. Caitlyn wanted to say something in response, but for some reason, she couldn't form the words. She simply sat and gazed at the man standing before her.

"I saw you sitting here all alone," came the voice again, somewhat more confident this time. "I was hoping you and I could dance."

Caitlyn smiled as she rose to her feet, hoping that her unspoken answer would serve as her consent. The two moved out onto the dance floor, but Caitlyn discovered she could hardly feel her feet beneath her. Her dance partner, although a man of few words, was light on his feet and led her about the room with obvious skill. While they danced, Caitlyn wanted to seek the answers to her questions: Who was he? Where did he live? Why had she not seen him before? She looked up at him as they stepped close. She took in the simple vest and trousers, his hat showing the wear of many days working outdoors. *He must be a farmer,* she concluded.

"I don't believe we've ever met," she said finally.

He looked down at her, his eyes seeming to take in every detail of her upturned face. There was something about those eyes that drew her. They were almost familiar, as if she had encountered them before.

"No, we've never met," he confirmed, whirling her around again.

"Are you new in town?" she persisted, once more gazing into the eyes she just couldn't resist.

"I suppose you could say that," he responded. "But we've been here for awhile."

"We?"

"My family and I," he responded.

"I'm sorry, but I don't recall your name," she continued. "I don't believe I introduced myself. My name is Caitlyn Schmidt. I'm the school teacher here."

"I know," he said, smiling ever so slightly. "How clumsy of me to forget to introduce myself. I'm—"

"Caitlyn." She was startled by the greeting as Rena tapped on her shoulder. "I'm so sorry to interrupt, but one of the parents is asking for you. They say they will be going home soon, but they have a few questions. Could you spare a few minutes?"

Caitlyn groaned inwardly. Why did such a perfect moment have to end so soon?

"Yes, tell them I'll be right there." She turned back to her dance partner with a regretful smile. "Thank you for the dance," she said softly. *Whoever you are,* her thoughts completed. She walked away without glancing back. Maybe he would ask her to dance again later.

But the rest of the social passed uneventfully. Caitlyn spoke with several parents and students before they departed for their homes. In the midst of all the farewells, the gentleman did not make another appearance. She resigned herself to the fact that he must have had to hurry home. She contented herself instead with the realization that she might see him again. He wouldn't have been at the school social unless he had some relationship to a student. Maybe he was the newest member on the school board. Either way, if he had come to the social, perhaps they would meet again.

Three

The Christmas holiday passed quickly for Caitlyn. She enjoyed attending the many services at church with her family, and there were the expected holiday treats: her ma's freshly baked sugar cookies dusted with white sugar and the Christmas ham, sweet and plump, cooked to perfection from Grandma's secret recipe. Of course there were presents, but like every Christmas, each gift was handmade and presented in love. Rena, Matthew, and Madeline joined the Schmidts for the Christmas festivities, and when the day drew to a close, Caitlyn bid her sister's family farewell. Now that winter had set in, it would be harder to travel, especially when the snow buried the roads in tall drifts. They might see one another at church on Sundays, but even the trip into town was difficult in the winter months. While the Schmidts lived on the western edge of town, the Fosters had built their farm to the south. In the summer months, the distance was not so great, but winter only made the distance seem unbearably long.

The first days of January brought heavy snow and strong winds. These conditions didn't let up for several days, the Schmidts forced to remain indoors, only venturing outside for chores in the barn or to retrieve melted snow for water. Caitlyn assisted her mother with the mending, cooking, and cleaning, but it wasn't long before the days' activities became mundane and tedious.

When the weather finally cleared, Caitlyn and her father shoveled a more accessible path from the house to the barn. The storm had dissipated in time for them to make plans to attend church the next day. The roads would be nearly impassable, but they were eager to get to town since they had been away for much of the preceding week.

Caitlyn dressed for church, shivering in her cold bedroom. She could see her breath in the icy air, and she

Beyond the Fury

hurried into her clothes as quickly as she could manage. As she pinned up her long, golden hair, she thought of the young man from the school social. Would he be at church today? Would he recognize her? Would he speak to her? With these questions foremost in her mind, she took extra care with her appearance, making sure her hair lay just so and that every wrinkle had been smoothed from her Sunday dress. She wanted to look her best, not only because it was Sunday, but also for the young man she hoped she would meet again.

Caitlyn's father hitched up the sleigh, while her mother gathered blankets and heated stones to keep them warm on the trip to church. Once on their way, Caitlyn took in the sights around her. Everything was covered with a crisp blanket of pure white. The leafless trees were also coated with the powdery snow, which glistened in the early morning sunlight. The light breeze, although accompanied by brilliant sunlight, did not carry a bit of warmth. *In fact,* Caitlyn thought, *it was downright cold.* Her nose felt as if it was frozen, and she wiggled her toes to get closer to the warmth of the heated stones. She moved closer to her mother as well, hoping that their closeness might also bring a measure of warmth.

"It's only January," Mrs. Schmidt remarked, "And I'm already looking forward to spring. I hope it will not stay cold like this for long."

"It's Wisconsin," her husband responded. "What else can you expect from winters here?"

"Yes, I know," Mrs. Schmidt said with a sigh. "But every year I seem to forget just how cold it gets."

"Spring will come," Caitlyn said. "One day we'll wake up and everything will be green and growing. That's the beauty of Wisconsin. You just never know when the weather will change."

"So true," her father said with a chuckle. "So true."

As if in answer to Caitlyn's prediction, less than two weeks later, the temperature warmed enough to lure Caitlyn outside. She breathed in the fresh scent of recently fallen snow and reveled in the late January sunlight. Although it would be rather chilly, Caitlyn already knew she wanted to ride. She was sure that Rena wouldn't mind a visitor. It had been two weeks since they had been to town, and she eagerly looked forward to a much-needed talk with her older sister.

"Ma," Caitlyn called as she reentered the house. "I'm going to ride out to Matthew and Rena's. I should be back by supper."

"All right," her mother responded from the parlor. "If you're sure. It isn't all that warm out there."

"I know," Caitlyn said, already anticipating the biting wind. "But I really want to go."

"Be careful then. I don't want your pa upset. You know how he doesn't like you to go out riding by yourself when it's this cold."

"I know, Ma," she said. "I'll be careful."

Once in the barn, Caitlyn saddled her favorite mare, taking great care in arranging everything before she mounted. She could tell the horse was eager to run, just as she was eager to ride. She smiled to herself in anticipation. It was days like these that made her wish spring would come soon. She mounted the horse and was soon on her way, the mare trotting down the pathway away from the barn. The chilly January breeze tossed her hair haphazardly around her shoulders as it escaped from the winter hat that struggled to hold the strands in place. Although the ride was accompanied by frigid winds, Caitlyn was simply glad to be outdoors again after being confined to the house for so long.

When she reached the Foster farm, she tied the reins to the hitching post and turned to the house. Rena met her at the door with a smile and invited her inside. Caitlyn breathed in the delightful smells of fresh apple pie and the remaining evidence of dinner. The kitchen table was strewn with pieces of calico, most likely the beginnings of one of Rena's many sewing endeavors. Madeline played with a rag doll on the rug in front of the window. The bright sunlight streamed in through the glass, creating a picture of contentment as the girl sat quietly playing.

"I didn't expect you today," Rena said as she led her sister further into the kitchen.

"I just decided that it was a beautiful day to go riding," Caitlyn replied as she knelt down to give Madeline a quick hug. "And how is my favorite little niece?"

Beyond the Fury

"Auntie Caitlyn," the girl said, holding up her doll. "Mama made this doll for me."

"Oh? Well, she's very pretty."

"She never had a doll of her own," Rena explained. "I wanted to give it to her on her birthday, but I just couldn't wait. She loves that doll so much and carries her everywhere. She calls it her 'Maddie doll.' She was determined to name the doll after herself, even though her pa and I suggested so many other names."

"She's so happy playing there," Caitlyn said, looking on wistfully.

"Someday Caitlyn, you will have children of your own," Rena assured her. "I'm sure it won't be long before you find that someone special."

Caitlyn sighed. "I'm just a typical school teacher; no men take interest in girls like me."

"Well, that man at the social certainly looked interested. I'm sorry I had to interrupt your dance. He was handsome."

Caitlyn smiled, feeling her face heat. "Yes, he was," she agreed.

"Had you ever seen him before?"

"No, at least I don't think so. He hardly said anything while we danced, and I never did learn his name. He was so quiet."

"Maybe he's just a little shy," Rena suggested.

"Maybe, but that doesn't keep me from wondering if I'll see him again. I've been hoping to find him at church, but every time we've attended since Christmas, he hasn't been there."

"Maybe he attends a different church," Rena suggested. "But either way, little sister, if you're meant to meet again, you will. Just give it some time. Oh, while you're here, why don't I make some tea? And you just have to see this new material Matthew brought from the milliner this past week. I've been piecing together a dress for Madeline…"

The brief spell of warm weather only lasted a few days. By the time Caitlyn returned to the school for the first day of the spring term, another heavy snowfall had buried the town and surrounding countryside with a heavy layer of white. Because of the deep drifts, many children who lived out into the country did not attend school that first day. Even with the small number of students, Caitlyn led the children in the day's activities. The children seemed eager to learn, and Caitlyn wasn't going to let this eagerness slip away. It would only be a matter of time before their young minds were diverted to something else.

As the next few weeks passed, Caitlyn began to fall back into her regular daily routine. She would rise early and help her mother with breakfast. It also wasn't uncommon for her to brave the cold mornings, offering her father help in the barn. Although the cold was enough to chill her to the bone, she would walk to school when the chores were completed and the breakfast dishes had been cleared away.

On one particular morning, Caitlyn could feel the cold seep into her bedroom even before she had fully awakened. The wind whistled around the corners of the house, and without even looking toward the window, Caitlyn knew it was snowing again. She dreaded leaving the warmth of the thick quilts wrapped tightly around her. With a groan of protest, she quickly slipped out of bed, her feet immediately seeking her thickest, wool stockings. She dressed in layers, knowing that on a day like this, a person would never be fully warm.

By the time she had made her way down from the loft, her father was just coming in from the barn.

"I was wondering if you were going to stay in bed all day," her mother said as she placed a steaming pot of oatmeal on the table.

"I'm sorry, Ma," Caitlyn said as she sat down in her usual chair. "It's just so cold. I wanted to stay where it was warm."

"Well, it feels like it's twenty below zero out there," her father remarked as he washed his hands in the basin by the cook stove. "I would think you wouldn't have to go to school today. The snow is coming down awfully hard, and the wind is cold enough to freeze a person right away. The parents would be crazy to send their children out on a day like this."

"I hope you're right, Pa," Caitlyn said as she dished up a helping of oatmeal. "I would hate for the children to come expecting school, and then I wouldn't be there."

Beyond the Fury

"Well, if it makes you feel better, Cait, I'll ride out to the school after breakfast and make sure no one's there waiting. If I see any of the children, I'll take them home myself."

"Thank you, Pa. I think it will be good to have a snow day. The children will love the idea, I'm sure, and I could use the day to mark those essays I've been meaning to read. It will be a good day for all of us I think."

That day was the first of many snow days over the next few weeks. On the rare occasion that the teacher and students were able to venture to the little schoolhouse, the drifts were so high that no lessons could be conducted until a path was cleared to the door. Often Caitlyn allowed the children to go home early when she saw the first snowflakes of an impending storm. She didn't want her students to be caught in the brutal elements for any period of time.

One morning as the children studied their reading lessons, Caitlyn found her mind wandering back to the night of the school social. As she looked around the room, the even rows of desks seemed to disappear as she recalled the open space that had been made for the dancing. What a night that had been! She couldn't forget the dance she had shared with the handsome man with the wavy, brown hair. She pictured his smile and the way his dark eyes seemed to mirror that smile as he had gazed at her. If only she could see him again! Then maybe she could ask his name and talk with him. There was so much she wanted to know!

But then she found reality. She hadn't seen him since that night, and based purely on this fact, it appeared that she might never see him again.

She was so deep in thought that it was remarkable she was able to pull herself back to the present. It was time for recess, but still much too cold for the children to play outdoors. She announced to the class that they were welcome to talk quietly amongst themselves or play a game. She was able to free herself from her thoughts long enough to grade a few arithmetic assignments, all the while keeping an eye on the children.

"Miss Schmidt." Elaina Torgeson approached the teacher's desk with a smile.

"Yes, Elaina."

"Mama asked me to give this to you," the girl said, extending a folded piece of paper toward Caitlyn. "I think she wants you to come for supper."

"That would be wonderful," Caitlyn responded, unfolding the single sheet. She quickly read over the neat script. Just as Elaina had said, it was indeed an invitation to supper for that very evening if Caitlyn had no other plans. The note told her that Mr. Torgeson would come for her with the wagon sometime before six o'clock. "Tell your ma I would be happy to join your family for supper," she said with a smile.

"Good. Mama will be so glad. I'll see you tonight then."

As promised, Henry Torgeson came for her around six o'clock. Darkness had already fallen over the countryside, and Caitlyn could see the first stars glimmer in a patch of clear sky overhead. It wasn't bitterly cold on this particular night, but yet, she was very glad for the warmth of her heavy coat.

Along the way, Caitlyn learned that the Torgesons had arrived in the area late in the summer, confirming what Elaina had told her. The family, which had originated in South Dakota, had decided to travel east for new farmland. Mr. Torgeson had high hopes for successful crops and a positive outlook for cattle raising.

"Most travel west from here," Caitlyn said at one point. "I'm surprised you came east to farm."

"Well, I think my boys said it best, Miss Schmidt. There's not much for farming beyond the Dakotas. Eventually, you'll end up in the mountains."

"I guess they know their geography."

"You've taught them well," Mr. Torgeson replied. "And they hardly ever complain about having to go to school." The horses slowed as the wagon lurched into a snow-roughened drive. "Well, here we are. My wife will be glad that I have delivered you safely."

He helped Caitlyn down from the wagon, and then led her to the door where Mrs. Torgeson greeted them with a wide smile.

"I'm so glad you could come," she said, reaching for Caitlyn's coat. As Caitlyn sat to remove her boots, she allowed her gaze to wander about the room. The kitchen was warm and bright, filled with the smells of pork and roasted potatoes. A cheery fire blazed in the cook stove, and fresh bread cooled on the table. Joseph and Anthony played in the adjoining room, chasing each other around the small space, giggling and squealing.

"May I help with anything?" Caitlyn asked as she stood from her chair, now free of her boots.

"No, dear, you just sit and enjoy yourself. I'm sure you're all tired out from those children at school."

"Thank you, Mrs. Torgeson. I—"

Her words were cut short as the door opened. Expecting Mr. Torgeson, Caitlyn was surprised to see someone else entirely. The door closed behind the newcomer as he removed his hat, revealing the wavy, brown hair she remembered so well. And when he turned toward her, she felt her quick intake of breath. It was him.

Four

Caitlyn stared in amazement at the man in front of her. Could it really be the man from the school social? Before she could even begin to formulate an answer to her unspoken question, she knew it was true. But why was he here?

"Miss Schmidt," Mrs. Torgeson said as she stepped forward. "This is our oldest son, James. I believe you have met before… at the social."

James turned to hang his hat on a hook by the door, and then approached Caitlyn with a smile. As he drew closer, he extended his hand.

"H-hello," Caitlyn stammered, mortified that she couldn't adequately form the words.

"It's good to see you again," he said as she placed her hand in his. His grasp was warm and firm, much like his father's, she observed.

"I'm glad to be here. Your mother was so kind to invite me." Caitlyn was relieved to be free of her earlier stutter.

"Supper is almost ready," Mrs. Torgeson said as she began bringing the food to the table. She then called to the children in the other room. When Mr. Torgeson returned to the house, they all sat down to eat. Mr. Torgeson led them in prayer, and the food was soon passed from hand to hand. Although the supper was delicious, Caitlyn found she cared little about her meal. She struggled to keep from glancing at James, but every time she caught her eyes wandering to his face, she saw him glancing her way as well. She would smile at him and return her eyes to the plate in front of her.

James's presence at the table did not completely dominate her evening. The others asked her about her teaching; Mr. Torgeson wanted to be sure that his sons and daughter were putting forward their best efforts in the

Beyond the Fury

classroom. Caitlyn assured him and his wife that the children were doing rather well.

"Right now, Elaina is at the top of her class," Caitlyn announced. "She has come so far since the beginning of the term. I've allowed her to start helping the younger children. Some of them need the individual attention that I just cannot give. Elaina is perfectly capable of helping them in their studies. Based on what I have seen from her, she could make a fine teacher someday if she wishes to pursue the education."

"Elaina, you didn't mention any of this," her mother said in surprise, glancing at her daughter. "We're so proud of you."

Elaina beamed with pride and turned her attention back to her supper.

After everyone had eaten and Caitlyn insisted she assist Mrs. Torgeson and Elaina in cleaning up the kitchen, they all moved into the main room of the farmhouse. Joseph and Anthony set up a game of checkers on the floor while Mrs. Torgeson took up her knitting and sat in the rocking chair in the corner. Mr. Torgeson sat near his wife on the couch, fully engrossed in the newspaper, occasionally glancing up to inform them of the town's most recent news. Elaina retrieved a book from her room and sat quietly reading. Caitlyn and James were left to sit on the remaining couch. As Mrs. Torgeson knit, she engaged the two young people in conversation, but as the evening wore on, the room fell into a peaceful quiet.

At one point, James stood and took down a small knife and a piece of wood. Caitlyn looked on with interest as he began carving into the soft wood, and after some time, she began to see the intricate formation of a decorative cross.

"It's beautiful," Caitlyn found herself saying as she reached out to touch the delicate design.

"Thank you," James replied, looking up momentarily to smile at her. "I just started work on it last night."

"You must have been doing this kind of work for a long time," she said, marveling at the intricate detail.

"Pa taught me when I was younger," he responded, continuing to move the knife over the wood.

"He's been perfecting his work for years," Mrs. Torgeson remarked. She gestured to the uppermost level of the bookshelf. "He carved all of those... except for a few. Henry did most of the larger ones."

Caitlyn stood to examine the display. The woodcarvings portrayed almost everything imaginable: flowers, animals, decorative shapes, human likenesses, and engraved lettering.

"You made all of these?" she said in amazement, turning back to the couch.

"Not all, remember," he said quietly. "Just a few."

"You could sell these in town," she responded, carefully lifting down a replica of a rose in full bloom. She lightly ran her fingers over its surface. But then she realized what she had done. What was she thinking, touching his work without his permission? Guiltily, she placed the carving back on the shelf, reluctant to turn back toward him. But at last she did, meeting his deep, brown eyes.

"I'm sorry," she mumbled. "I just got carried away with how beautiful everything is."

"It's all right," he replied in a voice barely audible. "I'm glad you like them all so much."

"I'm serious, Mr. Torgeson. You could make good money selling your work," she said softly, once more joining him on the couch.

James shook his head as he turned his gaze back to the cross in his hands. "No, this is just for fun," he told her. "My work is here with Pa on the farm." He looked up again, meeting her gaze for a brief moment. "And if you don't mind, please call me James. No more of this formality."

"All right then, James. Only if you agree to call me Caitlyn."

"Agreed," he said with a smile, and turned his attention back to his work.

Some time later, Caitlyn was astonished to discover that it was getting late. Mrs. Torgeson had begun to ready the youngest children for bed until all that remained in the main room were Mr. Torgeson, Elaina, James, and herself.

"Maybe we should think about getting you home," James said as he glanced at the clock.

"Oh, Miss Schmidt, I'm sorry," Mr. Torgeson said, rising from his chair. "Everyone was so quiet, I almost forgot you were here."

Caitlyn couldn't resist a laugh. "That's all right, Mr. Torgeson. But maybe I should be getting back."

"Pa, can I take her home?" James asked, glancing at Caitlyn as if to seek her permission as well.

"Sure, son. That's fine with me."

"Well, then, let's get your coat, and we'll be on our way," he said as they walked through the kitchen. James helped her into her coat, his closeness reminding her once more of the dance they had shared weeks earlier. She found herself looking forward to the ride home with him at her side. Perhaps they would finally get a chance to talk.

James asked her to wait inside while he hitched the team to the wagon. In that time, Mrs. Torgeson returned to the kitchen after tucking the children into bed. She thanked Caitlyn for coming, and in turn, Caitlyn thanked her hostess for the delicious meal and pleasant evening. Mrs. Torgeson invited her to come again soon, and thinking of James, Caitlyn quickly accepted.

James came to the door to lead her outside. It had snowed some during the evening, and the two carefully walked through the light powder that dusted the tops of their boots. Once in the wagon, they rode through the countryside in silence, but Caitlyn wanted to talk. Somewhat shyly, she spoke.

"Do you know where I live?" she asked, her quiet voice shattering the solitude.

"Pa and I talked about it in the barn earlier," James explained. "I think I can manage."

"Good," she said, burrowing deeper into her coat. The wind had picked up ever so slightly.

"You know," he said. "I've been thinking about the school social. I'm sorry we didn't get to finish our dance."

"I am too," she replied. "If my sister hadn't—"

"Oh, it wasn't her fault," James interjected. "You were needed. You're the teacher— people expect you to see to your duties."

"I know, but I'll admit, it was one time when I wish I didn't have such commitments."

"But you love to teach."

"Of course," she said quickly. "I have great students, which make it all worth it, especially children like Elaina and your brothers."

"I'm sorry I had to leave that night without saying goodbye."

"I looked for you," she admitted. "But I figured you just had to go. I had no idea you were a brother to Joseph, Anthony, and Elaina."

"That's my fault," James responded. "I never gave you my name."

"Well, that's behind us now," said Caitlyn. "Oh, that's our farm up ahead. You can pull in here."

The team and wagon soon came to a stop in front of the Schmidt house.

"Let me help you down," James said as he leaped from the wagon and reached up his hand to assist her. Safely on the ground, Caitlyn looked up at the man who stood in front of her. "Thank you for taking me home. I can get to the door just fine. Good night, Mr. Tor— James."

She turned toward the house, but she hesitated as James called her back. She retraced the few steps she had taken, once more standing in front of him.

"Sometime, if it would be all right with you... and your father, I'd like to call on you, Caitlyn."

Could she be hearing him correctly? But if what he was saying was true, she had no desire to abandon this opportunity.

"I'd like that," she said in response.

James tipped his hat to her, and then stepped up into the wagon again. "I will look forward to seeing you soon then," he said.

Caitlyn imagined that he smiled at her, even though his face was shadowed from her view in the pale moonlight. She raised a hand to wave as the horses trotted down the driveway. And with a smile of her own, she turned once more toward the house.

Five

Over the next few days, Caitlyn instructed her students in their studies, but all the while, she couldn't prevent a smile from continually springing to her lips. James Torgeson wanted to call on her, and she couldn't keep her excitement bottled inside. Seeing Elaina and her brothers every day only helped to remind her of their older brother. She eagerly waited for the day when he would arrive at their farm and speak with her father. The day couldn't seem to come quickly enough.

Nearly a week later, Caitlyn returned home from school one day to see an unfamiliar wagon in front of the house. She wondered who it could be. Could it be James? She resisted the urge to run to the house, but even so, she couldn't contain the excitement that had welled up inside of her. She opened the door to the house, hearing voices coming from the parlor.

"That must be her now," she heard her mother say. "Caitlyn, dear, please come into the parlor. There's someone here to see you."

Caitlyn deposited her books on the kitchen table and made her way to the parlor. She could detect her father's voice and another male voice responding to him.

"Miss Schmidt," the young man said as he rose from his chair.

"Caitlyn," she reminded him. "Please call me Caitlyn."

"Caitlyn," he said as he reached for her hand.

"I'm sorry I took so long at the school. If I would have known you would be here, I would have hurried home."

"I didn't even know I would be here," he replied. "There was a little break in the work at home, so I decided it was time to come and talk with your parents."

"Mr. Torgeson has just asked if he might call on you, Caitlyn," her father informed her.

Caitlyn glanced at James, and he met her gaze with a wink and a grin.

"What was your answer, Pa?" she asked, suddenly fearful of what he might say. What if he said no?

"Well, yes, of course," Pa said with a laugh. "It's about time my youngest daughter started thinking about her future. After all, Rena was married at your age."

Caitlyn looked up at James with another smile. She couldn't keep the happiness inside any longer.

"Now, Caitlyn, I'm sure you would agree in asking James to supper," her mother said. "Such an occasion is worthy of celebration." As she passed Caitlyn on her way to the kitchen, she whispered for Caitlyn's ears only, "My Cait has finally found someone special."

A few weeks later, the Schmidts and Fosters had another reason to celebrate: Madeline's fourth birthday. The family watched as Madeline opened her gifts: a new dress from her parents, a picture book from her grandparents, and an assortment of peppermints and other candy from Andrew. The little girl opened each gift with eagerness. Upon opening Caitlyn's present, she did a little dance about the room. She tore back the paper to reveal a miniature dress, pieced together just like the dress Rena had made, only this one was for her rag doll.

"Look, Maddie," Mr. Schmidt said as he reached out to hug the girl. "Now you and 'Maddie doll' can dress alike."

Madeline's smile was enough to cause the whole family to grin in response. For the rest of the day, she carried around her rag doll wearing the new dress. Her other gifts seemed to be neglected, except when she was reminded of her own matching dress.

"I must say, Caitlyn. That gift of yours went over quite well," Andrew said as he helped himself to a second piece of birthday cake at supper later that evening.

Caitlyn couldn't resist a grin. "I only wanted her to have something to play with. This way, she can dress her doll and have fun while doing it. It's all about being creative,

Beyond the Fury

Andrew. You've given her candy every year ever since she could eat solid food. She deserves some variety."

"But children love candy," Andrew objected as he took a bite of cake.

"Well, this year the doll dress won over," said Caitlyn with finality.

"What Caitlyn is trying to say is that Madeline likes her better than you," Rena said as she turned to Andrew.

"I said no such thing," Caitlyn exclaimed.

"But you were implying it, weren't you?" Andrew retorted.

"Come on, you two," Matthew intervened with a laugh. "Can't you get through one day without tearing into each other?"

"Oh, Matthew, you know it's all in fun," Caitlyn said with a grin. "Right, Andrew?"

"Sure," Andrew said with sarcasm. "How do you know I'm not being serious?"

"You're not, and I know that for a fact."

"Oh, really?"

"All right. That's enough," said Mrs. Schmidt. "You both fight like you could be brother and sister."

"Well, we *are* family, Mama… thanks to Rena and Matthew," Caitlyn responded.

"I give up," Mrs. Schmidt said as she reached for her coffee cup. "I could use some more coffee, Rena, if you've got any left."

"So," Rena said as she dried a plate and set it aside. Her blue eyes sparkled with excitement. "Where's this man of yours?"

Caitlyn rinsed a cup and handed it to her sister. "James is at home, why?"

"I thought you would invite him here for Madeline's party. After all, he is courting you."

"Today was for family. James would have felt horribly out of place. And besides, he and his father are cleaning out the barn today and getting ready for spring. It will be awhile before they will be able to get out into the fields, but every bit of work helps to get everything ready."

"How long has it been since you've seen him?" Rena asked, gathering the remaining silverware from the table.

"It's been a few weeks," Caitlyn replied. "He's been busy lately, but he invited me to dinner with his family after church tomorrow."

"I'm so happy for you, Caitlyn," said Rena, her eyes gleaming. "He's so handsome, so hardworking. He would take good care of you. Have you discussed the future?"

"Rena," she exclaimed. "We've only known each other a little while. You talk as if we should be married by now. Neither of us is ready for that."

"But maybe some day soon," her sister suggested. "I really think he's perfect for you, Caitlyn, and everyone else seems to think the same. When the time comes, you'll know. Just trust the Lord to lead you in the right direction."

Caitlyn nodded as she washed the last plate and handed it to Rena. "Enough of this serious talk," she said. "Let's get back to the party."

Six

The middle of March brought another heavy snow to New Richmond. For the first time in awhile, Caitlyn did not rejoice at the prospect of a few days away from the classroom. Although she was able to get ahead on some lesson plans, the heavy snow prevented James from coming to call. In the past few weeks, he had come almost every evening after completing his chores. Often he would bring his carving, and she would sit at his side, mending or crocheting as she watched him. As they grew better acquainted, James began to open up to her. They talked comfortably now about almost everything: his work on the farm, her teaching, and yes, even their future together.

During his last visit just a few days before the storm, James had surprised Caitlyn with his suggestion that they spend some time in town on their evenings together.

"I think we could have a lot of fun skating at the rink, or we could go to one of the Sunday night gatherings together. And there's still plenty of snow. We could go sledding if you'd like."

"That sounds wonderful, James," she said. "But why the sudden interest?"

"Well, I know some of your friends have been inviting you to join them in their fun, and here I've been taking up your every available evening."

"I don't mind," Caitlyn assured him.

"Well, either way, I think it's time we let everyone know that we're together… a couple. I wouldn't want any young men thinking you're available."

"You have nothing to worry about," Caitlyn said, looking up at him in complete seriousness. "Thanks to Rena, I think the whole town knows you've been coming to call on me."

The room was silent for a moment. Only the ticking of the parlor clock could be heard as James took Caitlyn's hand in his.

"There's something I've been meaning to ask you, Caitlyn," he said, his dark eyes conveying a deep earnestness. "I've grown to care for you greatly over the last few months, more than I've ever cared for anyone. You're very special to me, and there's no one I'd rather spend my time with. I can't give you everything, but I will do my best to provide for your needs."

"What are you saying, James?" she asked, the nature of his words catching her by surprise.

"I love you, Caitlyn, and I know we haven't known each other long, but there's one thing I know for sure; you and I are meant to share our lives together. Please, Caitlyn, consider your future, *our* future. Will you marry me and become my wife?"

Caitlyn's breath left her, and at first she thought she was dreaming. Could he really be proposing marriage? There was so much to consider. Was she ready to become his wife? Could she do everything Rena and her mother did? Could she manage a household, raise the children, and still provide her husband with the attention and love he deserved from her? How could she make such a decision so quickly?

"Caitlyn?" The deep brown eyes that scrutinized her were overflowing with love and understanding. He reached for her other hand, now clasping both of hers in his. His hands were warm and work-roughened, but yet so gentle. Caitlyn gazed deeply into his eyes, at last finding the courage to speak.

"There's so much to consider," she said softly, her voice wavering with the uncertainty she felt.

"I understand," he said, lightly stroking her cheek. "If you don't have an answer now, that's okay. There will be time to talk later. Just know that I love you."

Even in the midst of his overwhelming proposition, Caitlyn was certain about one thing.

"I love you too, James," she practically whispered. "I really do."

Seven

"Rena, what have I done?"

Caitlyn paced the main room of the Foster home, looking to her sister as if she could provide the answers she needed.

"It's not as if you said yes to his proposal," Rena pointed out.

"I know," Caitlyn responded. "But I almost did. He was so serious about everything. I could tell he really does have feelings for me. He says he loves me, but Rena, it's just too early for me to make such a decision. We've only known each other for a few months. I don't understand why he wants to hurry things along so much."

"Have you told him any of this?" Rena asked.

"Some," Caitlyn replied. "He seemed to understand, but I felt as if I were letting him down."

"If he really does love you, Caitlyn, he will respect your feelings. Why don't you think everything over for a few days? Maybe then you will be able to tell him how you feel."

Caitlyn nodded. "It's just so overwhelming right now. Was it this way when you and Matthew were discussing marriage?"

Rena laughed. "Oh, much worse. It seemed like forever before he proposed. I wanted him to ask me to be his wife, and it seemed like he just wanted to prolong our friendship. When he finally did propose, I could hardly believe it."

"I know it might sound crazy," Caitlyn continued. "But I really do love James… at least I think it's love. Maybe it's too early to tell, but being married to him…" Her voice trailed off.

"Just talk to him, Caitlyn. He'll understand."

Caitlyn sighed, and at last ceased her pacing. She sank down into a nearby chair, resting her head in her hands. It only took her a moment to consider.

"All right, I'll go talk to him. After all, it *is* Saturday. I don't have school, and he should be out at the farm."

Rena nodded in silent agreement.

"Thank you, Rena," Caitlyn said. "I don't know what I would do without you."

She quickly hugged her older sister and then turned toward the door.

Caitlyn jumped from the wagon and made her way toward the Torgesons' barn, hoping to find James. She opened the door and stepped inside, waiting a moment for her eyes to adjust to the dimness. The cows and horses turned to look at her as she slowly moved down the center row of stalls.

"James," she called softly, continuing on her way toward the back of the barn.

"Caitlyn, is that you?" came his answer from behind a large workhorse in the back corner.

She swallowed hard. Now that she had come, she didn't know what to say. Maybe she should turn back now while she had the chance. But she couldn't. She had promised Rena she would talk to him, and she knew that once everything was out in the open, both of them would feel so much better.

"Yes, it's me," Caitlyn replied, trying to banish the tremor in her voice.

James stepped into the center aisle, brushing bits of hay from his trousers.

"Well, this is a nice surprise," he said with a smile. His dark eyes seemed to brighten at the sight of her.

"James, we need to talk," she found herself saying suddenly. In a way, she regretted her abruptness, but deep down, she knew it was for the best.

He reached out to take her hand, his gloved fingers intertwining with hers. Without a word, he retrieved two milking stools and set them close together. Then he indicated that she should sit next to him.

"What is it, Caitlyn?" he asked, her hand still held securely in his. "Have you thought about what I said the other night?"

"Actually, yes; that's what I came to talk about," she said softly, at last finding the courage to meet his gaze. Ever since she had entered the barn she had found it difficult to look into his eyes, those wonderful eyes that seemed to detect everything about her.

"Do you have an answer for me?"

She shook her head without reply, trying to find the words to express how she felt. She took a deep breath and prayed for strength.

"I care for you, too, James and I know I have come to love you. But I don't know yet just how deep that love is. If we are going to be married, I need to know you better. I need to know for certain."

James nodded, seeming to carefully weigh her words.

"So you're not saying no?"

She nodded. "But I'm not saying yes either. I'm sorry, James."

She looked down at her lap in sudden shyness. What would James think of her now?

"Caitlyn," James said as he placed a finger under her chin and lifted her head, his gaze intent on hers. "I will wait until you are ready. Please know that I love you, and if I have to wait for years, I will. But Caitlyn, can you promise me just one thing?"

She nodded.

"Please consider me as part of your future."

She smiled at him with love welling up in her heart. "I promise," she whispered.

At first Caitlyn thought she and James were crazy. But as her mother frequently told her in the weeks to come, love did strange things to people. Even though she had only known James for a few months, it was as if they had known each other for years. They rarely had to explain anything to each other in great depth. He seemed to know what she was thinking and just how to respond. And the same was true for

Caitlyn. Just one look into the dark pools of his eyes, and she felt as if she had truly found the one with whom she was supposed to spend the rest of her life.

As the snow began to melt and the weather gradually warmed, Caitlyn did her best to concentrate on her teaching. But as the students completed their lessons, she often found her mind wandering to James. She did her best to brush such thoughts aside, telling herself that there would be plenty of time to daydream at home. But no matter how hard she tried, his face was always imprinted in her thoughts, his voice foremost in her mind's wanderings.

As Caitlyn prepared the children for final examinations, she was finally able to set aside her daydreams. Summer was coming, and there would be time to devote to daydreaming later. For now, she had to help the children in their studies. Because of the hard winter, many of the children were behind the other students in their schoolwork. Caitlyn did her best to bring everyone to the same level, but it was nearly impossible. She enlisted Elaina's help, and the two stayed long after the last bell every day, individually instructing those students that were struggling to keep up with the others.

On one particular afternoon in early May, Caitlyn reached to close the schoolroom windows, breathing in the fresh breezes of early spring.

"It's such a beautiful day," she said to Elaina as she closed the last window. "It's a shame to close everything up. Oh, Elaina, could you wipe down the chalkboard? Then we can head home."

"Are you coming for supper tonight, Miss Schmidt?" Elaina asked as she moved toward the door with the erasers.

"Well, your brother didn't invite me," Caitlyn said with a smile.

"What if I invited you?" she asked as she opened the door. Caitlyn could hear the clapping of the erasers as Elaina rid them of chalk dust. When she returned to the classroom, a mischievous smile tugged at the corners of her lips. "On second thought, I don't think I'll have to invite you."

"What do you mean?" Caitlyn asked. But even as she spoke, she could hear the approaching horses and clatter of a wagon drawing near to the school.

Elaina opened the schoolhouse door wider to reveal James stepping from the wagon.

Beyond the Fury

"Well, if it isn't my sister and her beautiful teacher," he said as he approached the doorway. "May I escort you two lovely ladies home for supper?"

Both girls laughed lightly, amused by his formality.

"Of course," Elaina answered for both of them, turning to her teacher with a contagious smile.

Supper that evening was delicious as always. Mrs. Torgeson sure knew how to please everyone in the kitchen. However, it was the end of the meal that both surprised and delighted Caitlyn. Mrs. Torgeson set a frosted chocolate cake in the center of the table, smiling at Caitlyn.

"Someone told us that your birthday is tomorrow," she said. "And we wanted to do something special for you."

"Thank you," Caitlyn responded. "But you didn't have to go through all this trouble."

"Everyone needs to celebrate their birthday," James said. "Besides, you've been working so hard at school. No doubt all those children will pass the term with excellent marks thanks to you and Elaina."

Caitlyn could only smile in gratitude.

"Here, Miss Schmidt. You can cut the cake," Elaina said, placing a knife in her hand. "You're going to love it. It's Mama's special recipe."

"I'm sure it's delicious," Caitlyn replied as she sliced the knife through the moist, spongy cake. When she had dished up a piece for everyone, she seated herself once more next to James. He flashed a quick smile and reached for her hand. Squeezing it lightly, he whispered, "Happy birthday, Caitlyn."

Later that evening, James and Caitlyn sat on the Torgesons' front porch. As the sun slipped behind the hill to the west of the farm, the warmth of the spring day began to gradually evaporate. James drew an arm around Caitlyn's shoulders as if he had sensed that she was cold. Caitlyn glanced up at him with unspoken gratitude, and nestled close to his side.

"It sure is a beautiful night," James remarked as he drew her even closer.

"Yes," she said softly. "And I'm sure you're praying for another nice day tomorrow. You need to get that planting in before it rains again."

"Not only that, but you deserve a beautiful birthday," he replied.

"The weather tomorrow will make no difference to me. I'll be at school all day, and then Mama needs my help to churn the butter. It'll be just another day."

"Now, don't say that," James objected as he rose from the bench. "Wait here. I'll be right back."

He vanished into the house for a moment, and when he returned, he carried a wrapped package. He extended the bundle out to her, and then resumed his seat at her side.

"Oh, James, you didn't have to get me anything," she said as she fiddled with the little white ribbon that held the wrapping in place.

"I couldn't let your birthday pass by without getting you something," James said, gesturing toward the gift. "Please open it."

"Who told you about my birthday?" Caitlyn asked, ignoring his urgings to open the package.

"Can't a man have some secrets?" came his response.

"Seriously, who told you?" she persisted.

"All right," he said in resignation. "If you must know, it was your sister. She mentioned it in church on Sunday. Now, please open it."

Without another word, Caitlyn untied the ribbon and pulled back the brown paper. As the folds fell away, her eye caught the glint of a shiny surface. Lifting the object out of its bed of paper, she discovered it was a small mirror. The wooden frame was engraved with tiny designs, hearts and flowers encircling the shiny glass.

"Oh, James, it's beautiful," she said quietly. "Did you make this yourself?"

"No," he said. "I can't take credit for that. Pa and I were in Minneapolis to get some supplies. I saw this, and I knew I had to get it for you."

"I'll think of you every time I look into the mirror. Thank you."

James bent his head to kiss her lightly, lingering close for a moment. "Since we can't be together tomorrow, I wanted tonight to be special for you."

"Oh, it's been wonderful, James, absolutely wonderful. I couldn't have asked for a better birthday, even if it is a day early."

Eight

"Good morning, Miss Schmidt," a woman greeted as Caitlyn entered the general store on Main Street. It was an overcast Saturday a few weeks later, and her mother had sent her into town for a few items. Caitlyn greeted the woman in return and moved toward the back of the store.

"Did you hear about the circus?"

Caitlyn found it hard to ignore the voice of Delores Hamilton, whom everyone knew as the town gossip. "It's going to be the biggest thing New Richmond has ever seen. There'll be lions and bears, and I think someone even said kangaroos. Oh, and don't forget the music."

"Are you talking about the Gollmar Brothers' Circus?" Grace O'Connor asked. Grace was one of Caitlyn's friends from grade school, and at the sound of her voice, Caitlyn couldn't resist joining the conversation.

"A circus is coming to town?" she asked, approaching the two women at the back of the store.

"Yes, dear," Mrs. Hamilton confirmed, her piercing green eyes, which never seemed to miss anything, glittered with an obvious excitement. "Won't your children at school have something to talk about now."

"Just what I need," Caitlyn said with a groan. But she couldn't suppress a smile. "They need to concentrate on their studies."

"Well, not with the circus coming to town," Grace replied. "Half the town knows already. No one can stop talking about it. There are posters hanging all over."

"When will it take place?" Caitlyn asked in interest.

"June 12," Mrs. Hamilton replied. "And from what I hear, there will be events all day. Oh, it's sure to be wonderful."

"Excuse me, ladies," Andrew Foster said as he made his way past them.

"Andrew," Caitlyn said with excitement. "Have you heard about the circus?"

"Oh, Miss Schmidt, I didn't see you there," Andrew replied as he turned back toward the women. "Yes, I heard talk of it. It's pretty exciting."

"It sure is. What brings you to the store today?" she asked as she lifted a sack of flour down from an upper shelf.

"I had to run some errands for the mill," he replied, relieving her of the heavy burden. "Here, let me bring this to the counter for you."

"Thank you," she said with a grateful smile. She then turned back to the women, catching the brief glances they shared between them.

"What?" Caitlyn asked, curiously taking in the display.

"Oh, nothing," Grace said, hiding a giggle behind her hand. "Nothing at all."

Caitlyn shrugged her shoulders and turned back to collect the remaining food and household items that her mother needed. She approached the counter, noticing that Andrew also stood in line.

"Done with your shopping, Miss Schmidt?" he asked, sending her a mischievous smile. For some reason, he thought it entertaining to address her as the children at school did.

"Yes, Mr. Foster," she said, returning his greeting. She made sure to strongly emphasize the 'Mr.'

"Having a good day?" he asked.

"Yes. You?"

"I can't complain. This circus business has everyone so excited; it's kind of hard not to join in. The children at school will be difficult to keep quiet after word about this gets out."

"Don't remind me," Caitlyn mumbled. "I guess I've got my work cut out for me."

"I'd say," Andrew agreed. "Come on. You should see one of those posters they put up."

They left their items to be purchased on the counter so they could venture outside. Just outside the general store, a large sign advertised the anticipated event:

COMING SOON!
GOLLMAR BROS.
Leading show of the world!
Two ring circus!
Menagerie and museum will exhibit at
NEW RICHMOND
JUNE 12TH
ONE TICKET AT HALF PRICE
25C admits to the big show.

The advertisement went on to tell about the exotic animals that would be present at the event, including Minnie, the smallest pony on earth, and Nero, the somersaulting dog. The poster promised a day filled with excitement for both young and old.

"Maddie will love this," Andrew said as they moved away from the poster, offering others the opportunity to look as well. "Maybe we can all go together."

"By then school will be over and we can celebrate the beginning of summer," Caitlyn agreed.

"Until then, I hope you can maintain order in the classroom," he said.

"Are you saying I'm not capable of handling my students?" Caitlyn asked.

"No, not at all." He looked at her with a seriousness that caught her by surprise. She had expected the usual rebuttal, the teasing, and the banter. "You're very good with your students, Caitlyn, and I'm sure everything will be fine. Just be prepared for a very animated group Monday morning."

Nine

    Caitlyn smiled proudly as Elaina Torgeson recited poetry from her English text, while the other students looked on, transfixed by her dramatic take on the short literary work. One by one, other students followed, presenting their examinations to the rest of the class. Some noticeably struggled, but Caitlyn didn't let this effect her nearly perfect day. It was a beautiful day outside, and a warm breeze wafted in through the schoolroom windows. The students were doing the best they could considering the previous winter and the continual excitement over the circus. Overall, today was special, and the day was far from over. As could be expected, the term would conclude with a social that evening, and the beautiful spring weather only served to bring anticipation for the event.

    As the afternoon came to a close, Caitlyn looked at the clock, realizing that there was still an hour of class time remaining. When she informed the students of this fact, many groaned. The parents that were present laughed, and Caitlyn smiled at her students, recognizing their hard work and accomplishments over the past term.

    "You have all done well today," she praised them. "And as a reward, you may all go home early."

    Cheers filled the room as desks were emptied and papers and books collected. Caitlyn said goodbye to her students and their parents, promising to see many of them that evening. The classroom emptied of all but one student— Elaina— and Caitlyn approached the girl where she tidied the books on the shelf.

    "Elaina, you may go home now. There's no need for you to stay."

    "I guess it's just habit," she said, turning to her teacher with a smile. "If you want me to go, I will."

"Oh, I'm not asking you to leave," Caitlyn replied. "But wouldn't you rather be out playing with the others?" Even as they spoke, they could hear the exuberant voices of children as they ran around outside.

"No, I thought I'd just look for a few books to read over the summer if that's okay," she said.

"Sure, that's fine, Elaina. You're always reading, aren't you? And you've been such a big help this past term. I don't know what I would have done without you."

"Thank you, Miss Schmidt," she said with a smile as she turned back to the books. Once more, the child brushed off her compliments, humbly going back to the task at hand. But Caitlyn hardly had time to contemplate the matter before she heard a familiar voice at the door.

"Good afternoon, Caitlyn," James said as he entered the schoolhouse.

"Hello, James," she replied with a smile, moving toward him. When she drew near, he pulled her close for a quick kiss. It was then that he must have realized Elaina was in the room, for he turned to his sister with an impatient smile.

"Elaina, shouldn't you be home by now?" he asked, his gaze fixed on Caitlyn as he continued to hold her close.

When the girl didn't respond, James glanced over at his sister, his look of impatience quickly replaced by a glare.

"Do you think you could leave your teacher and me alone for a few minutes?" he tried again. "It's important, Elaina."

Elaina continued to examine the books on the shelf, seeming to pay no heed to her brother's words.

"Elaina."

This time the girl turned at the sound of her brother's commanding tone. Book in hand, she turned from the bookshelf and made her way toward the door. Caitlyn didn't miss the secretive little smile that Elaina tried to hide behind her hand. When the door closed behind her, James gathered Caitlyn close again.

"James, what's going on?" Caitlyn asked, trying to hold back her laughter.

"Nothing really," he replied. "Can't I simply come to walk you home?"

"Of course," she responded with an eager smile.

"And ask if I might escort you to the social tonight?"

Beyond the Fury

"That would be wonderful," she said. Seeing the serious look in his eyes, she suddenly sensed there was more to his schoolroom visit. "Is there anything else?" she found herself asking.

"Well, actually..."

"Yes?"

"Caitlyn," he began, his voice soft. "I've decided that I can't wait any longer. I've come to ask you to be my wife. Please say you'll marry me."

Caitlyn looked up into his deep, brown eyes, which were filled with so much love, it would have been impossible for her to turn away. And without a doubt, the answer came, her voice confident and sure.

"Yes, James. Yes, I'll marry you."

His smile was enough to weaken her at the knees. She would have fainted at the level of joy that welled in her if James hadn't lifted her off the ground, spinning her around in seemingly endless circles. Their laughter echoed off the schoolroom walls.

"Did she say yes?" came a child's voice from the door. "Did she?" Elaina ran to them, her eyes bright with eagerness.

James couldn't resist a kiss from his bride-to-be even as Elaina tugged at his sleeve.

"What did she say?" the girl's voice came again.

"What does it look like to you, little sister?" James asked, grasping Caitlyn's hand as he turned them both to face Elaina.

"She must have said yes," Elaina concluded.

Caitlyn held out an arm to the girl, beckoning Elaina to come closer. James moved in between them, drawing an arm around both their shoulders.

"We'd best get you home so you can get ready for the social," he said to Caitlyn.

Ten

The still evening air hung over the Torgeson farm as Caitlyn and James sat together on the front porch. Both were silent, but for Caitlyn, their companionable quiet was comforting. The past few days had been absolutely wonderful. It felt as if her engagement to James were a dream come true. Everything was happening so quickly, and for the first time since Thursday afternoon, Caitlyn finally felt as if the world had slowed enough for her to take a deep breath and simply sit, taking in the beauty of the June evening.

Seeming to sense her contentment, James drew her close, allowing her to rest her head on his shoulder. "What are you thinking about?" he asked softly.

She let out her breath slowly in a sigh, gazing up at him with a slight smile. The lamps inside the kitchen window cast a golden glow over his face, his dark eyes now intent on hers.

"You... us..." she said quietly, fumbling for the right words. "I can't believe that we'll be married in just a few months. August seems so far away, but yet it's so close. I can't wait."

He smiled at her as he took her hand. "Neither can I," he responded. "You've made me the happiest man around, Caitlyn. God has truly blessed me with your love."

"I think He's blessed me more," she contradicted mildly. "I love you, James."

"The feeling is mutual, Caitlyn."

At that moment, they heard the bells from the Catholic church in town as they chimed the hour. The faint breeze carried the joyful sound across the countryside, immediately confirming in Caitlyn just how perfect everything had turned out to be.

"You know it's a clear night when you can hear the bells," James said after awhile as the music faded into the still night air.

Caitlyn nodded in reply, not wanting to shatter the quiet beauty of the moment. "It's getting late," she mumbled reluctantly. "There's so much to do tomorrow with the circus and everything. And now there's a wedding to plan too. Rena and I are going to start piecing together my dress in the morning, so maybe I should be getting home."

"Of course," James responded, rising from the bench and helping her to her feet. "I'm sorry to have kept you so late. I just didn't want the day to end."

"Me neither," she agreed as he led her down the porch steps and toward the wagon. "If there was such a thing as a perfect day, today would have been it. The picnic was wonderful. Thank you for everything, James. I had such a good time."

"I did too," he said as he assisted her up into the wagon. "And hopefully tomorrow will be just as wonderful. Are you looking forward to the circus?"

"Who isn't?" Caitlyn said as he joined her in the wagon. "I'm so glad we'll be able to go together."

"Oh, that reminds me," James said as he flicked the reins. "Would you mind riding into town with your family tomorrow?"

"No, I wouldn't mind. Why?"

"Well, Pa and I have quite a bit to do on the farm tomorrow, and I want to get a good start on my work before I head to town. If you went with your family, you wouldn't have to miss any of the circus. I would make sure to be in town by noon. I'm sorry to—"

"It's fine, James," she said, catching his eye. "As long as you can find us when you get to town, it will all work out."

"Thank you for understanding, my Caitlyn," he said, a relieved smile spreading across his face. "I promise to make it up to you."

Caitlyn loved it when he addressed her as his— *my Caitlyn*. It served to remind her that in just a few short weeks, she would truly be his and he would be her husband.

"Oh, Rena," Caitlyn breathed in wonder. "It's absolutely perfect."

Caitlyn ran her hand over the length of the white taffeta as she glanced up at her sister with a smile. "I can't believe you found this here in New Richmond. I didn't think there would be anything so fine in town."

"I didn't either," her sister responded. "But when I saw this on Saturday, I just knew you would want it."

Caitlyn smiled again, imagining the wedding dress that she and her sister would soon piece together. She thought of the tiny buttons, the delicate lace, and the intricate trim. Of course, it would take some time before the dress would reach such a level of completion, but Caitlyn eagerly looked forward to the day when she would walk down the aisle of the church, the elegant gown trailing behind her. She anticipated the look in James's eyes as she met him at the altar, his gaze full of love and adoration.

"Caitlyn," came her sister's voice. Caitlyn looked up, startled out of her thoughts. "You were daydreaming."

"I'm sorry," she said, her cheeks flushed with embarrassment. "Should we get to work?"

"I'm ready if you are," Rena said with a teasing smile, her bright blue eyes glittering. "That is if you can keep your head out of the clouds."

Caitlyn couldn't resist a laugh as she retrieved a handkerchief from her apron pocket. Dabbing at her sweat-dampened forehead she said, "I can't believe how hot it is today, and it's not even ten o'clock yet. Why, there's not even a breeze, and to think, summer hasn't even officially begun." She moved toward the kitchen window, gazing out on the abnormally warm June day.

"But at least it's warm," Rena remarked, joining her sister at the window. She attempted to fan herself with her own handkerchief. "I don't even want to remember this past winter. I can't recall another time when it was that cold."

"We can truly be thankful that summer has finally come," Caitlyn replied. She leaned closer to the open window, hoping to catch even the slightest breeze.

"I've been meaning to ask you," Rena began. "What will you do this summer now that school is done?"

"I don't know for sure," she answered. "There is so much to do before the wedding. August will come rather quickly. I should also plan ahead for next term. Since I won't be teaching after the wedding, I would like to leave the new teacher with some ideas regarding the children's progress so they can continue in their studies. Some of the students are excelling far beyond what I expected, and I want to be sure that they will be challenged. Oh, that reminds me; I had planned to stop by the school today to pick up a few things. James came to walk me home from school on Thursday, so I didn't get a chance to organize everything. I guess you could say I was a little distracted."

Rena smiled knowingly. "With the circus and everything going on today, will you even have time?" she asked. "Besides, aren't you and James meeting in town later? Can't the work wait until tomorrow?"

Caitlyn sighed. "I suppose you're right. There will be plenty of time for schoolwork later. When did you all plan on heading to town?"

"Around noon," Rena replied. "You wanted to ride with us, right?"

"Yes, if that's okay with you and Matthew."

"Of course. The more the merrier. Andrew asked if he could join us as well. He should be here shortly."

"Isn't he needed at the sawmill today?" Caitlyn asked. But it didn't take her long to recall Andrew's earlier eagerness in getting the opportunity to spend the day with the family. He had already promised little Madeline ice cream as a treat in addition to the circus festivities.

"Fortunately, he has the day off," Rena confirmed as she turned from the window. She unfolded some of the taffeta and draped it over the kitchen table. "Many of the workers wanted the day to spend with their families, but someone has to run the mill. Andrew has the day free though, and no doubt, he'll spoil Madeline rotten."

"That's a given," Caitlyn responded with a grin. "Now enough of this talk. Let's get working on my dress."

But Caitlyn didn't immediately hurry to her sister's side. For a moment, she stood at the window, taking in the beauty of the June morning. Vibrant blue sky stretched over the Wisconsin countryside as far as she could see, the late morning sun spreading its warmth over the recently planted fields. The people of New Richmond couldn't have asked for a more perfect day for the highly anticipated circus. It was sure to be a wonderful afternoon, and all in all, it promised to be a day to remember.

"Caitlyn," Rena said. "If you want to get started…"

"Yes," she said, at last turning from the window. "I'm coming."

The two worked quietly, cutting and laying out the material as if they knew what the other intended to do. After awhile, they set aside the unfinished gown to prepare for the noon meal. They would be eating a little earlier so they would be ready to leave for town. As they prepared the leftover chicken and fresh bread, they heard a commotion at the door.

"Mama! Mama!" Madeline cried as she ran into the room. "Uncle Andrew's here! Papa's coming!"

Caitlyn turned from setting out dishes to smile at the child. "Maddie, come help me," she said, holding out a plate and cup to the girl. Madeline hurried toward her in eagerness, and the two made quick work of setting the table.

Moments later, Matthew and Andrew came into the kitchen, and the family sat down to eat. In their hurry to head for town, the meal only took a few minutes. As Rena and Caitlyn cleared the table, Matthew offered to hitch up the team and wagon so they could leave as soon as the women finished their work in the kitchen.

"So Caitlyn," Andrew said as he lifted Madeline from her chair. "I thought you'd have other plans today… what with James and your… engagement."

She had to struggle to hide a smile. Lately, it seemed her family was having difficulty becoming accustomed to her newly established relationship. They had all accepted James into the family circle, but now with her engagement, Caitlyn sensed a change in everyone, especially where Andrew was concerned. While everyone had expressed their congratulations and hopes for a long and prosperous marriage, a level of uncertainty had seemed to settle over everyone, Andrew in particular. She contented herself with the fact that this was simply a time of adjustment for everyone, including herself, and soon everything would return to some form of normalcy.

"James and I plan to meet in town later," Caitlyn replied as she approached Andrew and Madeline. She held out her arms for the little girl. She proceeded to gently wipe Madeline's face with a damp cloth, all evidences of the child's dinner soon a thing of the past. "Now you're all pretty for the circus, Maddie." She placed Madeline on the floor, and almost immediately, the girl began to run around the room, squealing excitedly.

"Circus time! Circus time! We're going to the circus!"

"That's right, Maddie," Andrew said as he reached for the child's hand. "Let's get you in the wagon so we can leave soon." He then looked to Caitlyn as if to question her plans.

"Yes, I'll be coming too," she said. "Just give me a minute to help Rena get everything ready. You can go ahead and get Madeline settled. We'll be out shortly."

He nodded and scooped Madeline up into his arms. The child giggled and chatted animatedly as Andrew carried her to the wagon. Moments later, Rena and Caitlyn joined Matthew, Andrew, and Madeline, and they were soon on their way. It didn't take them long to reach town, and as they made their way down Main Street, Caitlyn noted how New Richmond seemed to practically buzz with activity. Already, large groups of people were gathering outside the storefronts. Buggies and carriages lined the sides of the street, horses tied to nearby hitching posts. The stores were congested with dozens of customers, all eager to purchase any necessary items before the afternoon festivities. Milk and baking carts were moving about on their daily routes, while the Roller Mill ground its flour.

But in addition to the ordinary routine, there was an element of anticipation in the air. At the far end of Main Street, circus workers were readying for the day's events while children, barely able to contain their excitement, ran about with their friends, refusing to heed their parents' commands to stay close.

In the back of the wagon, Caitlyn turned to Rena. "I can't believe how many people are here," she said.

"I know," Rena agreed. "I don't think I've ever seen so many people in one place before."

"I don't know if James will be able to find us in this crowd," Caitlyn remarked as she took in the activity going on around them.

"Did you plan to meet in any particular place?"

Caitlyn shook her head. "I'm just hoping he'll see us somewhere along the parade route."

Andrew maneuvered the horses around milling groups of people and other carriages and wagons. At one point, their wagon narrowly averted a collision with a mail cart crossing in front of them.

"Look, there's a nice place up ahead," Matthew said as the horses plodded along. "Andrew, why don't you see to the horses? I'll help everyone get situated."

Andrew reined in the horses, the wagon coming to rest in front of the shoe store.

"Perfect!" Rena exclaimed with a smile as she fanned herself with her handkerchief. "And it's even in the shade."

"That was the intent," Matthew said with a grin. "Is this all right with everyone else?"

Caitlyn and Andrew nodded their agreement, and then the two men jumped down from the wagon. Andrew offered his hand to Rena in an effort to help her down, but she shook her head. "We might as well stay in the wagon," she said. "We'll be able to see really well from up here. There's no sense in climbing down."

"But wouldn't you like to walk around for awhile?" Matthew asked.

"No, not really," she replied, wiping her forehead with her handkerchief. "It's far too warm for that. Besides, I wouldn't want Maddie to get lost in the crowd."

"I'll walk," Caitlyn said, glancing over at her sister as if to ask her permission. "That is if it's okay with you, Rena. James will be looking for me soon anyway."

"I need to settle some things with my account at the bank," said Andrew. "You can come with me if you'd like."

"Sure," Caitlyn responded.

She stood and allowed Andrew to help her from the wagon. She then looped her arm through his, and together they made their way down the street. Neither of them spoke as they neared the bank. Caitlyn wanted to say something, but she couldn't find the words. She and Andrew hadn't talked for quite a few days, in fact, not since the announcement of her engagement. Their silence this afternoon seemed somehow awkward, as if neither one knew how to go about relating to the other. Something had obviously changed between them, for Caitlyn realized that their easy sense of camaraderie had suddenly disappeared.

Beyond the Fury

At the bank, Caitlyn waited near the door while Andrew completed his transaction. When he was through with his work at the desk and had signed the necessary papers, he rejoined her at the entrance and they emerged outside once more. Caitlyn blinked at the sudden brightness from the blazing sun, and she squinted her eyes shut for a brief moment. In the midst of the activity and bustle around them, an approaching horse and rider somehow caught her attention.

"It's Elaina," Caitlyn said to Andrew, spotting James's sister entering the bank lot on her brother's horse. "Maybe she knows something about James. He should be in town by now."

Elaina dismounted easily and brushed dust from her skirt, reaching up a hand to right her bonnet which had been knocked askew. "Oh, Caitlyn," she said in greeting. "I'm glad I found you. James sent me."

"Is everything all right?" Caitlyn asked.

"Everything's fine," Elaina said. "But James said you should go to the circus without him. He and Pa are having trouble birthing a calf, and he doesn't think he'll be able to come to town at all today."

"Oh," said Caitlyn, disappointment filling her. *Today was supposed to be perfect,* she thought, *and already plans were falling through.*

"I'm sorry," Elaina said.

"It's not your fault," Caitlyn assured her. "Are you going to the circus?"

Elaina shook her head. "Mama needs me at home today," she said.

"But it's the event of the summer," Caitlyn objected. "And you're going to miss it."

"I know," Elaina said softly. The girl was clearly disappointed. "I need to be getting back to the house now. I promised Mama I'd only be gone for a little while."

"All right, Elaina. Thank you for letting me know about James," Caitlyn responded. "Please say hello to him and the rest of your family for me."

"I will," Elaina promised as Andrew helped her into the saddle. Soon horse and rider disappeared down the street.

"Well, I guess it's just you and me," Andrew said, turning to Caitlyn with a smile. He once more extended his arm to her, and she accepted it with a smile of her own. "Why don't we go join Matthew, Rena, and Maddie?"

Caitlyn agreed and they made their way back to sit with the family.

Despite James's absence, Caitlyn had to admit that the afternoon was absolutely wonderful. She thoroughly enjoyed the circus, but no one seemed to enjoy the day more than Madeline. The little girl's eyes lit up with wonder as the parade of exotic animals passed in front of them. Her eyes widened at the sight of the ferocious lions, and she marveled at their large size. She giggled when Andrew pointed out the kangaroos and the stunts presented by the performing dogs.

"They hop, hop, hop," Madeline said in reference to the kangaroos as she scampered down from her mother's lap. She imitated the creatures as she jumped around the wagon, triggering laughter from the adults.

Performing bears passed the wagon next, followed by more specially trained dogs and horses.

"That must be Minnie," said Caitlyn, directing everyone's attention to the miniature pony moving in front of them. "The posters said that she's the smallest pony on earth."

"Look, Maddie," said Andrew as he gestured toward the horse. "That pony is little, just like you."

Madeline grinned as her gaze followed the horse and the other animals as they continued to proceed down the street. As the circus progressed, she became even more fascinated by the magic acts and mimes that danced about, the clowns' white faces bright in the afternoon sun.

"Look, Mama!" the child cried excitedly. "Tall person."

"Yes," Rena said, allowing the girl to stand on her lap so she could have a better view of the performance. "He's on stilts."

"Stilts," Madeline repeated, trying out the word on her tongue. "He's up high." She looked up at the man towering over her, her eyes wide.

Caitlyn and Andrew exchanged amused glances, the child's contagious excitement impossible to ignore.

Beyond the Fury

"Look at the juggler, Maddie," Matthew said, diverting the child's attention. "See how he catches all those balls and then throws them up in the air again?"

Madeline's eyes followed the movement of the bright balls as they danced between the juggler's hands. Throughout the entire event, Madeline was in a completely different world, captivated by every aspect of the circus. And when it was all over, Matthew carried a sleeping Madeline to the wagon.

"Rena, I think I'll see to those things you've been needing from the dry-goods store," Matthew told his wife, placing the sleeping child in her arms. "Why don't you stay here with Maddie? I'll only be a few minutes."

"Well, I'm sorry to run off too," Andrew said. "But I need to get a few things at the general store. Can I meet you back here later?"

"Sure, Andrew," Caitlyn responded. "We'll see you later then."

Andrew waved as he turned to go, and Caitlyn returned the gesture with a smile.

Matthew turned to go into the nearby dry-goods store as Rena made sure Madeline was comfortable in the back of the wagon.

"She'll be sleeping for a few hours for sure," Rena whispered. "She's got to be exhausted."

"Maddie had a great time today," Caitlyn said. "It was so much fun seeing her reaction to everything. She'll remember today for a long time."

"Definitely," her sister replied.

"Caitlyn, Rena, hello!"

The girls turned in the wagon seat to see their parents' wagon approaching from down the street.

"It's Ma and Pa," Caitlyn said, standing and waving. "I wonder what they want."

"How wonderful to see you," Mrs. Schmidt called out as the girls' father reined in the horses so the teams stood parallel to each other. "Did you have a good time at the circus?"

"We had a great time," Caitlyn responded. "Madeline is completely worn out from all the excitement."

"I can see that," Madeline's grandmother said with a smile, glancing toward the sleeping child. "Didn't Matthew and Andrew come with you?"

Rena nodded. "Matthew's inside," she said, waving her hand toward the store. "He'll be out in a few minutes. And Andrew's at the general store."

"I hope you are all planning to head home soon," Mr. Schmidt said as he looked to the sky. "It's getting awfully dark. It looks like it could rain. Caitlyn, maybe you'd better come home with us now."

For the first time, Caitlyn took notice of the clouds gathering on the southwest horizon. It had been such a beautiful day, but yet oppressively hot. Perhaps the rain would bring welcome relief from the heat.

She glanced back at her parents as her mother said, "Well, since you're all here in town together, why don't you come over for supper? I can cook up something simple."

"Sure," Caitlyn agreed. "That sounds great."

"I need to wait for Matthew," Rena replied. "And Andrew said he'd meet us here when he was through at the general store. Besides, Madeline is fast asleep. I think it would be best if we just head home. Sorry, Ma. Maybe we can have supper with you another time."

"That's fine, Rena. We understand," Mrs. Schmidt replied. She turned to Caitlyn. "Will you still join us?"

"Of course. I can come home with you now if you'd like."

"You're welcome to come then," her father said. "But we'd better hurry. It looks like the rain will be here soon."

Eleven

"Ma, do you want me to slice up some cheese? I've got the bread ready."

"Sure, Caitlyn. I'll be there to help you in a minute," Mrs. Schmidt responded.

Caitlyn proceeded to cut thin slices of cheese to add to the bread and butter that would become their evening meal. All the while, she thought over the events of the day, and what a day it had been! She and Rena had gotten a good start on her wedding dress, and Caitlyn knew that it would be absolutely beautiful once it was completed. Rena was quite talented when it came to sewing, especially intricate stitching. Caitlyn also recalled the time spent with family and friends. She regretted that the Torgesons hadn't been able to join them. She had been looking forward to spending the day with James in particular. Oh, how he, his brothers, and Elaina would have enjoyed the circus! But there had been work to do on the farm, and it seemed that the Torgesons never took a day to just simply relax. There was always the milking, crops, and machinery to fix. True, James relieved himself of work in the evenings when he came to call on her, but even so, Caitlyn felt he was working too hard.

Caitlyn placed the sandwiches on three waiting plates, and then carried them to the kitchen table. As she set out the cups and forks, her mind wandered back to the circus. Madeline had loved every minute of it, and Caitlyn smiled to herself as she remembered the child's excitement over the animals and magical performances. The circus had a way of bringing out the inner child in everyone. Caitlyn had observed Andrew as he interacted with Madeline. He made sure his niece didn't miss any part of the circus parade, and Caitlyn saw his obvious joy as he spoiled the girl with ice cream and a ride on his shoulders whenever she requested, "Up! Up!"

While outwardly, Andrew portrayed the eagerness of a child, Caitlyn had sensed that something wasn't right. Although he had interacted with the family as if everything was fine, Caitlyn knew he was struggling with something. They had always been able to converse so easily, but the past few days had revealed a kind of tension between them. Andrew spoke to her as if he were hesitant, almost as if he were uncomfortable in her presence. But it had never been like this before. What had changed, and why was Andrew acting so strangely? Vaguely, she associated the awkward state with her recent engagement, but she couldn't understand why such a thought had entered her head.

Caitlyn heard her mother's footsteps outside the kitchen, and she was startled back to the present.

"You were daydreaming again, weren't you?" Mrs. Schmidt said as she entered the room. Her gleaming eyes told Caitlyn she was aware of her wandering thoughts.

Caitlyn smiled sheepishly and turned her gaze to their supper.

"Looks like you've got everything ready," her mother said, taking a quick moment to survey Caitlyn's work. "Why don't you call for your pa, and I'll get some milk from the ice box."

"Pa," Caitlyn called, leaving the kitchen and walking toward the parlor. "Supper's on the table."

As she neared the room, Caitlyn could hear the wind pick up outside. She was quickly reminded of the approaching rainstorm, and she anticipated the cooling shower. She lifted a corner of her apron to wipe the moisture from her damp face for what seemed like the hundredth time that day. With thoughts of rain and cooler temperatures, Caitlyn went into the parlor. The room was dim, the two windows facing the south revealing ominous clouds threatening outside.

As she moved further into the room, Caitlyn spotted her father sitting in his favorite chair, the piece of furniture turned ever so slightly so he could face the windows. Caitlyn stepped to his side, immediately wondering about what had him so fascinated. Always intrigued by the weather, her father could often be found observing the approach of a summer storm, and today was no exception.

"Pa?"

Beyond the Fury

"Looks like it will be a bad one," he said, turning from the window. "I've never seen clouds like this."

Caitlyn moved closer to his chair, leaning to look out of the window. Outside, dark, thick clouds rolled over the landscape, churning and spinning as the wind seemed to push them along on an unknown course. The clouds hung low over the ground, so close that there hardly seemed a separation between where the green of the fields ended and the sky began. As the two watched from the window, a light rain began to fall, gradually growing in intensity until the raindrops pelted heavily against the windowpanes and roof. Then it was as if the raindrops had become ice pellets, clattering down upon the house with increasing force.

"Hail," her father said in explanation. "The wind's picking up too."

Caitlyn's gaze was fixed intently outside the rain-splattered window. The sky had suddenly taken on a mysterious, yellow-green hue, and the trees surrounding the house swayed crazily back and forth in the strengthening wind. The scene outside was strange and eerie. This storm was unlike any she had ever seen before, and what she saw next caused her to cry out.

"Pa, w-what is that?"

Her father leaned close to the glass, his gaze seeming captivated by the threatening sky. A large, funnel-shaped column extended toward the ground and hovered over the distant horizon. The massive cloud dipped lower, and dust and dirt swirled in the air. The deluge of rain and hail let up for a moment, and in the lull, Caitlyn heard an unmistakable roar.

"Pa?" Caitlyn's voice quivered.

"It's a cyclone," her father said, his gaze remaining fixed on the irregular cloud formation. "And it looks to be heading straight for town."

Twelve

Caitlyn couldn't bear to look any longer. She covered her face with her hands and sank into the chair that her father had since abandoned. "Ma!" she called, even though she knew it would be impossible for her mother to hear her over the howling winds. "Come quick!"

But there was no response from the kitchen. Fearful, Caitlyn once more turned toward the window. She had willed the impending storm to vanish, but at the sight of the increasingly darkened sky, Caitlyn shivered with dread, her whole body sensing the severity of the wind's force.

"Pa," she said tremulously. "Is it going to come for us too? Shouldn't we go to the storm cellar?"

"No, Cait," he said reassuringly. He placed a steadying hand on her shoulder. "The storm looks to be moving to the north of us. We'll be safe."

Relief filled her, and she relaxed against the chair with a sigh. But suddenly, she was hit with a renewed sense of dread, and it shook her to her very core.

"Rena! Madeline!" she exclaimed, rising from the chair so abruptly that it rocked crazily back and forth. "And Matthew and Andrew! They were still in town!"

"Oh, Father God," he murmured. "Not Rena! Oh, God, please protect them."

"Ma!" Caitlyn screamed, this time hurrying toward the kitchen. "Rena! The storm!"

"Caitlyn," her mother said, her voice strangely calm. She came from the kitchen at the sound of her daughter's cries. "What's the matter?"

By this time, Caitlyn was nearly hysterical, tears running unchecked down her cheeks. She frantically pointed toward the window, unable to find the words to adequately

Beyond the Fury

explain the scene unfolding outside. Mrs. Schmidt said nothing as she moved to stand at her husband's side.

Flashes of light dotted the horizon as the cyclone moved off to the north and east. Debris swirled up into the thick blackness, and although town was a great distance from the house, they could see roofs, tree limbs, and complete buildings as they were lifted into the churning sky and then hurled to the ground. Caitlyn thought she even caught a glimpse of a wagon hurtling through the air, a cow or horse not far behind.

As the three stood in silence, Caitlyn watched as the massive funnel rose from the ground, spinning in a circular motion overhead. It seemed to loom over the town below with imminent violence, threatening to drop from the sky once more without a moment's notice. They watched as the swirling mass merged with the oppressive storm clouds in the distance and gradually disappeared.

At last, the three tore their gazes from the window and looked at each other, too stunned to speak. As a sudden torrent of heavy rain slashed against the windows, Caitlyn's father reached for his wife and held her close, drawing Caitlyn to his side as well. And in the midst of the storm's fury, they waited, unwilling to accept the harsh reality that waited for them beyond the driving rain.

A light mist fell as Mr. and Mrs. Schmidt and Caitlyn emerged from the house. No one had spoken since they silently witnessed the storm's rage as it was enacted upon the town. Caitlyn found herself shaking with fear. What had become of New Richmond and its people? What had happened to Rena, Matthew, and the rest of their family? Then there was the outlying countryside to consider. How had the Fosters' farm fared, and had the Torgesons made it through the storm without serious consequences? Were James and his family safe?

"I think I'll ride into town to see what needs to be done," Mr. Schmidt said, his voice bringing her out of her reverie. "From the looks of it, there may be people trapped, and they'll need all the help they can get."

"Maybe I should gather up some blankets, food, and other supplies," Caitlyn's mother suggested. "There may be several that are injured."

Mr. Schmidt nodded. "Yes, Emily. Caitlyn, go and help your mother. I'll be ready to leave in a few minutes."

"Could I go with you, Pa?" Caitlyn asked, suddenly finding her voice. She felt the prodding need to accompany him to town, hoping that she could be of some assistance to the people. No doubt Rena and her family were among those that had experienced the horrors of the storm, and Caitlyn wanted to be certain they had escaped unharmed.

Her father shook his head. "Not now," he said. "We don't know the extent of what has happened."

"Please Pa," Caitlyn pleaded. "Let me go with you."

"No, Caitlyn; it's too dangerous. There's a lot of damage, and many of the buildings will be unstable. You could get hurt," her father said, saddling one of the horses.

"But what about Rena?" Caitlyn objected. "What if something happened to her? What about Matthew and Madeline?" Her voice faltered as once again, tears gathered in her eyes.

"I'll make sure to get word to you and your ma as soon as I know anything," he said, now astride the horse.

"Please Pa," Caitlyn tried again. "The people in town will need help. I'm sure of it. There were so many people on the streets when we left. Please, let me go with you, Pa."

"Thomas," Caitlyn's mother said, moving to stand beside her daughter. "Caitlyn's right. Many people are probably hurt and they will need help. It may be dangerous, but God will go with you. I will stay here at the house, and if anyone needs anything, I'll be able to help them. If you see Rena and Matthew… anyone, send them here."

Caitlyn's parents exchanged brief glances before her father finally consented.

"All right," he said, offering Caitlyn his hand. Making sure she was seated properly behind him, he lifted a hand toward his wife in silent farewell. As the horse trotted down the road, Caitlyn couldn't help but question what they would find in town. Judging by the storm's appearance, the damage would be extensive, and she immediately began to fear the worst. Her jumbled thoughts organized themselves into a desperate prayer; "Please, God, let everything be all right."

Thirteen

As they neared town, her thoughts were stilled as she looked around in disbelief. The roadside was strewn with broken tree limbs, and full trees torn from their roots now obstructed the path in front of them. Shingles, bits of tree bark, and wood splinters littered the ground as well, hindering their progress. As they drew closer to the town ahead, Caitlyn could detect the mingled odors of smoke and moist earth. The combined scent was a constant reminder of the uncertainty that awaited them.

As they entered the town limits, Caitlyn saw a young man running toward them. His shirt and trousers were badly torn, and blood trickled from his face. As he continued to run, he waved his hands in the air as if to halt their approach. In compliance, Mr. Schmidt reined in the horse. Expecting that the man would direct them in which way to go, Caitlyn was surprised when he hurried past them.

"Sir," her father called. "How are things in New Richmond? How has the town fared?"

But the man kept running, and as Caitlyn and her father continued on their way, others ran past them as well. Some wept as they fled town, their clothes and hair covered with mud and debris and streaming with blood. Their faces displayed the obvious horror they had seen, and Caitlyn wondered just how severe the damage was.

She didn't have long to contemplate the matter, for as the horse stepped around piles of rock, bricks, and broken boards, Caitlyn could see that very little remained. Buildings had literally been flattened, windows shattered, and broken plaster seemed to cover everything like a layer of thick dust. Horses whinnied and moved restlessly, hindered by minimal space and heavy debris. Many were still tied to the hitching posts where they had been left before the storm; others were tangled in rope or wire. Caitlyn witnessed one horse's struggle to free himself from a mass of telegraph wires, and when his efforts proved futile, he let out a whimper as if in despair.

Main Street, which was earlier filled with eager locals and visitors, was now almost unrecognizable. Wooden beams and bricks were strewn everywhere, the roadway a mass of mud, standing water, and unidentifiable objects that had been tossed about by the storm. Despite the recent downpours, black smoke billowed over the heavily damaged structures, orange flames licking at the displaced remnants of walls and roofs. Screams shattered the eerie calm that had settled over the town. Men hurried about, struggling to lift heavy beams from those trapped beneath collapsed buildings, while women stood shivering in their rain-soaked clothing, looking on as they gathered their children close.

Caitlyn tried to determine where they were, what buildings they were passing, but every previous landmark had been dashed into pieces and flattened into the ground. She managed to identify the church her family attended, and she was relieved to see that damage to the structure was not significant. Several yards past the church, she saw the church bell in the middle of the street, now free of its tower and layered with mud, wood splinters, and other debris.

"Help! Someone please help me!"

Caitlyn startled at the sound of the masculine screams. She was unable to see the man, but she could hear his cries with distinct clarity as they echoed in the still air. Up ahead, flames glowed in a demolished structure, and then she saw him— the owner of the pleading cries. Only his head was exposed amidst the shards of glass, shavings of wood, and scattered brick. The fire blazed fiercely mere inches from his trapped form, and Caitlyn shuddered as she heard his voice again.

"My leg! My leg!" he screamed.

Three men struggled to lift a fallen chimney from the man's body, which only caused his cries of pain to increase in frequency and volume. The chimney was removed, but even so, the man continued to cry out, saying that his leg was trapped under something heavy. The men that had come to his aid hurried to free him of the cumbersome debris, but Caitlyn could tell that time was quickly running out. She watched as the hungry flames steadily devoured everything around him, inching closer to his helpless form.

"Just cut it off!" The man's desperation tore at Caitlyn's heart as he pleaded for his life. He would rather they amputate his leg than leave him to the mercy of the flames. She leaned against her father's back as sudden tears brimmed in her eyes. She was powerless to help the man, and as his cries to be freed came once more, she closed her eyes at the realization that the man's entrapment was sure to lead to imminent death.

His rescuers persisted, but as the flames increased in intensity, the men began to desert, the fire consuming what was left of the structure. The man's cries were swallowed as the entire building was engulfed. Caitlyn couldn't prevent the tears that spilled from her eyes. If only they had been able to save him in time!

Caitlyn was sure she couldn't bear to see anything more. But as the horse continued to move forward, slowed by the destruction along the street, Caitlyn caught a glimpse of a child, and it was the most heart-wrenching scene she had ever laid eyes on. The young girl, not much older than Elaina, huddled on the exposed stairs of her home's storm cellar. She cradled a younger child in her arms, rocking him back and forth. The girl was hysterical, tears coursing down her cheeks as she held fast to the baby.

"He's dead," she sobbed, her swollen eyes meeting Caitlyn's across the piles of rubble. "My baby brother!"

It was then that Caitlyn recognized the girl. It was Sarah Kingsley, one of her students. She longed to jump from the horse so she could hold the girl close. She looked so forlorn, sitting there all alone. Where were her parents? Why didn't they come to comfort her?

"Pa, she needs me," Caitlyn said, her gaze never leaving the weeping child.

Her father turned toward her, his eyes implying his consent. He dismounted and lifted her to the ground. She stepped over a large timber in the middle of the street, nearly falling when her feet came in contact with a patch of mud. The wet earth clung to her shoes as her father reached for her arm to steady her. Caitlyn reached the girl in a few steps. Sarah looked up at her teacher, her eyes glazed with held-in tears and something else that Caitlyn couldn't define. Caitlyn said nothing as she lifted the baby from the girl's arms, instantly noting the limp form that she held. A quick check of his vital signs revealed that the baby was indeed dead. She wrapped the boy more securely in the blanket that surrounded his lifeless body, obscuring his face from Sarah's view.

"He's dead, isn't he?" came the girl's choked voice.

Caitlyn nodded. "I'm sorry, Sarah." She cradled the baby in one arm while she reached out to Sarah with her other hand.

Sarah's eyes welled up with fresh tears, but she brushed them away. She held out her arms for the baby, but Caitlyn shook her head.

"There's nothing more we can do, Sarah," she told her. "Where are your ma and pa?"

"Away," the child answered simply, the word catching on her tears. "They went to Hudson... Pa needed some supplies for the store."

Caitlyn gently drew the girl away from the cellar, leading her toward their horse. She looked up at her father with an unspoken question.

"We'll take her with us," he responded. "Although I'm not sure where to go." He took the baby from her arms so she could get settled on the horse. He then helped Sarah to sit behind her. The girl's arms went about Caitlyn's waist as she held on tight. The horse then proceeded to move forward, led by Mr. Schmidt who walked alongside them. At that moment, two men hurried past, carrying a young woman stretched out on a door now free of its hinges.

"We'll take her to the school," one man said to the other. "I hear they're taking the injured there."

Caitlyn strained to catch a glimpse of the young woman's face, terrified that it might be Rena— unconscious, bloodied, and bruised. But the girl and her rescuers hurried by, and Caitlyn took in a shuddering breath. She must remain calm. Sarah needed her to be strong.

"Why don't I take you to the school?" Caitlyn's father suggested. "Then I can come back here to help."

Caitlyn nodded, too overwhelmed to say anything in return.

Fourteen

The scene in the schoolhouse was chaotic— people rushing about, the injured moaning and crying out from their places on the muddied floor. Frantic mothers searched for their missing children and babies cried, their arms flailing helplessly. In the height of the activity around her, Caitlyn remembered her young charge, and she led the girl over to a desk. She expressed her reluctance at having to leave her, but Sarah seemed to understand that there were people that needed help. Caitlyn knew the child was striving to be brave, although her eyes brimmed with tears.

"Wait here," Caitlyn told her. "I'll see what needs to be done."

Caitlyn rose to her feet and assessed the situation before her. In a matter of moments, she spotted one of the town's physicians and hurried toward him.

"Doc Ryberg," she said breathlessly.

"Oh, Miss Schmidt," he said, turning toward her without his usual smile. His face was ghostly pale, and one look into his troubled, gray eyes and she knew he was just as overwhelmed as she. "Is there something I can do for you?"

Caitlyn shook her head, although she longed to express her worries for her sister's family. "I'm wondering if there is something I could do here. I know I don't have any medical training but—"

"We can certainly use you," the doctor interjected. "If you could, just make sure everyone is comfortable until I can see to them. Some of them are hurt badly, so you might have to stop their bleeding. We've gathered some sheets from the clinic, so you can use those for bandages if you need to. All of the clinics in town have been badly damaged, so supplies are limited. Even the sheets must be cut and used sparingly."

Caitlyn nodded.

"If you need me at any time, I won't be far away. Just call," he said as he turned to a patient lying nearby.

Caitlyn didn't waste any time before seeing to her appointed duties. She moved from one patient to another, asking if they had any pain and bandaging serious wounds. Some of the injuries were fairly routine— cuts and minor fractures. But when Caitlyn was presented with injuries that were more life altering in nature, she began to grasp just how severe the storm had been.

An older man cried out, complaining of a pain in his head. A little girl screamed and cried as Caitlyn did her best to remove particles of sand and dirt from her eyes. She nearly paled at the sight of a young man, a piece of steel protruding from his leg at a dangerous angle. The object could not be removed without the doctor's expertise, so until Doctor Ryberg could be made available, the man lost a great deal of blood.

As time went on, the injured continued to arrive, brought to the schoolhouse by those who had rescued them from beneath the ruins. Caitlyn, Sarah, and a few others continued to do all they could, compressing and bandaging wounds and readying patients for the doctor. All the while, Caitlyn didn't see anyone she knew among the injured. She prayed this might prove that her friends and family had escaped harm. She tried not to dwell on such thoughts, for the more she contemplated her personal situation, the more distracted she became from her work. God was watching over those she loved, and she contented herself with the knowledge that no matter what would come, His will was perfect.

She turned from a sleeping patient to greet the newest arrival. The woman looked vaguely familiar, but her face was almost unrecognizable due to the numerous cuts and lacerations that streamed with blood. But as soon as the woman spoke, Caitlyn knew without a doubt who lay in front of her.

"My nose, Miss Caitlyn," said Delores Hamilton. "I think it's broken."

"Well, we'll take a look at it and see what we can do," Caitlyn replied as she helped the woman to sit at one of the unoccupied desks. She dipped a rag in a nearby bucket of water and gently dabbed at the woman's face, careful not to touch her nose. Mrs. Hamilton winced as Caitlyn cleaned a cut on her chin, and the woman closed her eyes against the pain. Caitlyn saw a few tears escape from beneath her lashes, and she immediately assumed she had hurt her.

"I'm sorry, Mrs. Hamilton," she said as she turned to wring out the cloth over the bucket.

"Oh, my dear, it isn't you. You haven't hurt me." She dashed at the persistent tears with the back of her hand. "It's just that I can't bear the thought of my Avery..."

Caitlyn hesitated in her work and turned back toward her patient. "What is it, Mrs. Hamilton? What's happened?"

She heard the woman's shaky intake of breath. "We didn't have time to get to the cellar," Mrs. Hamilton practically whispered. Caitlyn had never heard her speak so softly. "At the last second, Avery lay over me, protecting me. He reached for my hand, and he told me that he loved me, but I could hardly hear him, it was so loud. Something hit me on the head and I didn't wake up for quite awhile. When they pulled me out, Avery was still next to me, holding my hand." She sniffed back tears and concluded, "He died right there, Miss Caitlyn, and I couldn't help him."

Caitlyn gently touched the woman's shoulder, unsure of how to respond. "Oh, Mrs. Hamilton," she managed to whisper. "I'm so sorry."

"Thank you, child, but I'll be all right," she replied, a hint of the usual spark returning to her eyes. Even her voice seemed a bit steadier. "There is work to do now, so we mustn't cry. There will be time for tears later."

Caitlyn nodded in silent sympathy. If only there were something she could do to comfort Mrs. Hamilton. How painful it must be to lose the one you loved! She couldn't begin to imagine what the woman must be experiencing at that moment.

"Miss Schmidt," someone called from across the room. "We need your help."

Caitlyn rose from tending to Mrs. Hamilton and hurried across the room. A middle-aged woman was brought into the room, lying on a makeshift stretcher. The woman was so badly burned that there was hardly an inch of her body that hadn't been touched by the flames. She moaned in pain, and it was obvious that she was barely conscious.

"Bring her over here," Caitlyn directed, and the two men carrying her deposited her gently on the floor. With

Caitlyn's assistance, they managed to remove the stretcher from beneath her, carrying the wooden plank with them when they left the schoolhouse. Caitlyn knew that just as medical supplies were limited, so were the means for transporting the injured. She turned for a brief moment to enlist Sarah's help, and when the two moved to kneel on either side of the woman, they witnessed her last ragged breath.

"She's passed on," Caitlyn said softly, unable to hold the tears at bay. How much more death did this child need to see? Caitlyn cried out to God in silent protest. Why did so many have to die? Would they be able to help all of the injured?

Caitlyn took Sarah's hand and led her away from the deceased woman. With a deep heaviness in her heart, she resumed her care of the other injured. She comforted worried mothers who were too injured to see to the needs of their children. She managed to quiet the screams of the frightened little ones, many of whom, only days before had left this very schoolhouse in anticipation of summer vacation. She was tending to one boy from the second grade class when she glanced up for a brief moment. Darkness had fallen outside, and for the first time, she took notice of the lanterns and candles that dimly illuminated the room. It was then that she saw Andrew Foster coming toward her, and in his arms he carried a small child.

"Caitlyn," he said as he approached, his voice hoarse with raw emotion.

"Andrew," she said, swallowing hard. She hadn't seen him since they had gone their separate ways after the circus, and she was relieved to see him standing in front of her unharmed. He and the child were covered with mud, and water dripped from Andrew's drenched shirt, making a puddle at his feet.

"Here, I'll take her," Caitlyn said, holding out her arms for the little girl. But Andrew turned away from her, seeming to clutch the child closer to his chest.

"What's wrong?" Caitlyn asked, moving closer to him. And then in disbelief, she recognized the little girl he held. It was Madeline.

"I found her at the dry-goods store," he explained, his eyes damp with what Caitlyn knew to be tears. "The building had collapsed and a wall had fallen on her. I've tried to wake her, but she appears to be unconscious."

Caitlyn reached for the child again, and reluctantly Andrew released his charge. Caitlyn gazed down at her unresponsive niece. The little girl's face and hair were caked with mud, a deep cut on her forehead oozing with blood. Caitlyn tore a corner from a sheet and dipped it in cool water. Dabbing at the wound, she glanced up to find Andrew hovering over her.

"Rena and Matthew," he said softly. "They didn't make it."

Caitlyn's hand stilled on Madeline's forehead, and she grasped the corner of a nearby desk for stability. "Rena... dead?" she whispered, choking on the words.

Andrew nodded, reaching out a hand to gently touch her shoulder. "They must have taken refuge in the dry-goods store before the storm hit. They were on either side of Madeline, trying to shield her." He took a deep breath, steadying his voice.

She turned away, resuming her care of Madeline. But all the while, she couldn't shake free of the thought: Rena was gone, and along with her, Andrew's own brother.

She gently cleaned the cut on Madeline's forehead, looking upon the child with a sudden sense of duty. Who would see to Madeline's care? In her sister's absence, she must make sure that Madeline was given everything she needed, this night and beyond. Madeline needed her, and she wouldn't leave the child's side for a moment.

Sensing his presence beside her, she turned to find Andrew still standing close.

"Will you look after Madeline for awhile?" he asked. "I'm going to Hudson to get help. Telephones don't work and telegraph wires are down all over town. We need medical supplies, doctors, more people to search for survivors..."

Caitlyn nodded. "Of course," she said softly. "I'll stay right here with her."

"Thank you, Caitlyn," he said, his eyes moist once more. "I may not see you for a few days... I hope Madeline will pull through."

"Oh, she will... I pray she will."

Fifteen

Hours passed while Caitlyn tended to Madeline and the other injured. Night had fallen over the schoolhouse, and despite her fatigue, she kept busy. There were so many to care for, and at times the task seemed overwhelming. If only there were more people to help with those that were hurt. She tried to grasp the severity of the situation at hand, but even so, her thoughts continued to return to Matthew and Rena. And what about James? How had he and his family fared during the storm? There were so many thoughts racing through her mind that she found it nearly impossible to concentrate on each new task. If only she could voice her thoughts to someone who would understand!

In the midst of the chaos and uncertainty, Caitlyn was relieved when she looked up to see her mother weaving her way through the maze of desks and people lying on the floor.

"Mama!" she cried, flinging herself into her arms. Her eyes welled with tears and she found she could hardly speak.

"Oh, Cait," her mother said, holding her close.

Caitlyn sniffed back tears, recalling Mrs. Hamilton's words. She wouldn't cry. But held securely in her mother's arms, Caitlyn felt a great release, and she couldn't prevent the rush of emotion that spilled forth. "Rena's gone," she sobbed.

"I know," Mrs. Schmidt said soothingly, stroking her daughter's hair and drawing her even closer. "Your pa told me."

"But how did he—"

"Andrew was there when Rena and Matthew were pulled out of the dry-goods store," she responded, wiping away a tear. "He told your father just a few minutes ago."

"Andrew found me here," Caitlyn whispered. "He told me... And Madeline—" Her voice caught on surfacing tears. She stepped away from her mother, wiping at her eyes. She laid a gentle hand on Madeline's hair, her fingers running through the tangled curls.

"Has she regained consciousness?" Mrs. Schmidt asked, moving to stand at her granddaughter's side.

Caitlyn shook her head, her eyes misting with tears.

"Then we will wait," her mother said simply, lowering herself to the floor. "I'll sit with her for awhile. Why don't you get some rest?"

"I can't possibly sleep," Caitlyn mumbled, her gaze on the child's sleeping form. "She needs me."

"But if you don't rest now, you'll be too tired to be of much help to anyone. It's nearly morning already, and there will be much to do tomorrow. I'll watch over Madeline and the others, and I'll wake you if anything changes."

Reluctantly, Caitlyn sank to the floor next to Madeline. She removed her coat and pillowed her head on its folds. As her mother hovered nearby, she allowed herself to close her eyes to the bustle around her. She released a shaky breath, rolling to her side. The wooden floor was far from comfortable, but it was the only option in the crowded room. She had no intention of sleeping, but she knew she must rest. She wanted to be able to give Madeline her full attention whenever she awoke. There was so much to consider and so much that couldn't be explained. She wanted to cry, once more longing to release the pent-up emotion, but she found it nearly impossible this time. Part of her couldn't seem to face reality. She wished she could turn back time, but the truth made itself known every time she turned to check on Madeline. Rena and Matthew— both of them gone. Why had all of this happened? She tried to pray, but she couldn't find the words.

"Please God," she whispered. "Please help us."

She buried her face in her coat, cushioning her head against the floor. She hoped that at morning's light, this nightmare would be over.

Golden sunlight filtered in through the shattered windows of the schoolhouse, rousing Caitlyn from a restless slumber. How had she managed to fall asleep? There was so much to be done, so many people who needed her help. She lifted her head from the floor, looking about for any signs of movement. Doc Ryberg paced the room, monitoring those still scattered about the floor. She heard the occasional murmur of his deep voice as he conversed with his patients while the rest of the room was immersed in a listless silence. Her mother was nowhere to be seen, and Caitlyn assumed she was caring for one of the many patients. Rising to her feet, Caitlyn looked down on Madeline, reaching out a hand to touch the child's matted hair. Just the sight of her bruised face and bloodied clothing caused her to turn away. The natural light of morning revealed the severity of her injuries, which had not been completely visible the night before. It was so unfair! Madeline lay young and defenseless, completely unaware of her future. She would never see her mother and father again, and because of this, her life would be forever changed.

With sudden realization, Caitlyn knew the same was true for her. Her sister, so vibrant and energetic, would never again brighten a room with her infectious smile and sparkling, blue eyes. Caitlyn looked on their time spent together as something that could never be replaced, and she found herself weeping for the older sister she had loved as a dear friend.

She knelt on the floor beside Madeline and buried her face in her hands, fully succumbing to the tears that threatened. At last she allowed herself to cry, releasing everything that she had held inside herself. She cried for Rena and Matthew, overtaken by the pain of their absence. She cried for Madeline and all of the children now left without the guidance of parents. And she cried for the town, now faced with the daunting task of recovery.

Caitlyn at last dried her eyes and rose to her feet, her uncertain steps carrying her to the schoolhouse door. Splintered and warped by the storm's strong winds, the door groaned in protest as she pushed against it. Now standing outside, Caitlyn was immediately greeted by the evidence of the storm's wrath. In the soft glow of the rising sun, the devastation almost seemed unreal. She took a deep breath, doing her best to banish any last remnants of tears and lifted her face to the sun's increasing warmth.

It was then that she realized she was no longer alone.

"Caitlyn?"

She turned to see Andrew making his way toward her.

"I thought you were going to ride to Hudson," she said.

"We've been back for a few hours," he replied, now standing close. "I wanted to see how you and Madeline were getting along."

"Madeline appears to be doing as well as can be expected," she told him. "Although I'm not sure if she's awakened yet. I haven't spoken to anyone this morning."

"I'll be praying that she'll come around soon," Andrew responded, reaching out to touch her shoulder. "And you, Caitlyn? How are you?"

Caitlyn looked away from him for a moment, again overcome by the existence of this harsh reality. "I don't know," she said, her voice trembling. "I just don't know."

Andrew drew an arm around her shoulders, and she felt her eyes filling with tears once more.

"What will we do now?" she asked, struggling to maintain her composure.

"We will rebuild," he said. "That's all we *can* do. Things will be different now— for all of us. But with God's help, we can face the future— whatever it may bring."

Caitlyn looked up at him, marveling at the confidence in his hopeful words. His sky blue eyes seemed to hold a promise in their gaze, and for a moment, Caitlyn felt a quiet peace settle over her.

"We will get through this," she whispered. "We'll start over."

Andrew nodded. "But it certainly won't be easy."

Caitlyn didn't reply as Andrew drew her close to his side again. She leaned against him and closed her eyes, wishing with all her heart that she could return to the day before or even weeks earlier, a time when things were as they should be.

"Caitlyn?"

She turned to see Sarah Kingsley standing at the schoolhouse door. She was smiling, and Caitlyn realized it was the first smile she had seen from anyone in the past few hours. "Your mother has been looking for you. She says Madeline is awake."

Caitlyn glanced at Andrew, catching the hopeful gleam in his eyes. In a sudden burst of eagerness, she reached for his arm, drawing him toward the school. "Come," she said. "We must see how she's feeling."

Andrew shook his head, reluctantly pulling free of her grasp. "I can't," he said. "I really need to be going. There is so much to do. I'd like to see her now, but Caitlyn—"

She met his piercing blue gaze, momentarily halted in mid-step.

"Please do everything you can for her," he implored.

"You know I will," she said. "I'll do my best."

She turned back toward the schoolhouse, following Sarah inside. Mrs. Schmidt met them at the door with a wide smile.

"How is she?" Caitlyn asked anxiously.

"Awake but in a lot of pain," came the answer. "She says her head hurts, and she hasn't been able to open her eyes."

Caitlyn hurried to kneel at Madeline's side. "Maddie?" she said softly.

The girl's eyelashes fluttered, but she did not open her eyes. She mumbled something incoherent.

"It's Auntie Caitlyn, Maddie. How are you feeling?"

"My head," she murmured, her tiny voice tinged with pain. Caitlyn stroked the golden curls back from the child's forehead.

"Has Doc Ryberg seen her?" Caitlyn asked, turning to her mother and Sarah.

"Yes, just a few minutes ago," Mrs. Schmidt replied. "He says there's nothing more that can be done for her. As long as she's comfortable…"

"Couldn't we take her home?" Caitlyn wondered aloud. "To our house, I mean. Wouldn't she be more comfortable there?"

"Doc doesn't advise moving her," Mrs. Schmidt replied. "At least not yet."

"Has she had anything to eat or drink? She'll need to get her strength back."

Mrs. Schmidt laid a hand on her daughter's shoulder. "She's too weak to eat at this point, but we've given her some water. She'll be fine, Caitlyn. Everyone has been taking good care of her."

Beyond the Fury

Caitlyn nodded, glancing over at Madeline again. If only the child would have escaped the storm without injury! It pained her to see the little girl so weak and helpless.

"A train from Chippewa Falls came late last night," Mrs. Schmidt said. Her sudden change of discussion momentarily caught Caitlyn by surprise. "They brought ten doctors and several nurses. And even more trains are scheduled to arrive in the next few days. By as early as tonight, we may have the expert help we need."

Again Caitlyn nodded. "I'm not leaving Madeline," she said softly.

"No one said you had to, dear," her mother replied gently. "There is still quite a good deal to be done. There is food to prepare, people to feed, supplies to organize... And the men will be occupied with the building. We will need some shelter in town, even if it is temporary."

Caitlyn contemplated all that her mother said. The tasks seemed so daunting. Would they be able to accomplish everything, to reconstruct New Richmond, to return the people to good health and strength? There was so much to consider...

"Would you ladies care for some biscuits? I'm sure you are quite hungry. And there's coffee too."

The women turned to acknowledge the Red Cross nurse who stood near them with a tray of biscuits extended out to them. Mrs. Schmidt and Sarah each accepted a biscuit from the tray, but Caitlyn shook her head.

"Caitlyn, you need to eat," her mother said.

Caitlyn knew it was true. She hadn't eaten since the hurried meal the previous afternoon at Matthew and Rena's. But the thought of her deceased sister and brother-in-law caused her stomach to churn with the sudden wrenching pain of their loss. She couldn't possibly think of eating now.

"I'm not hungry," she mumbled, turning away.

"All right," the nurse said with a friendly smile. "If you're sure."

Caitlyn nodded, and the nurse left to retrieve the coffee. Caitlyn glanced toward the door for a brief moment, watching as doctors, nurses, and even those less seriously injured entered and exited the room. In the midst of the activity by the door, Caitlyn was sure she saw Elaina Torgeson in the mass of people. It only took Caitlyn a moment to be certain. It *was* Elaina, and Mrs. Torgeson stood off to the side of the door, her hands on the girl's shoulders.

"Elaina?" Caitlyn said, leaving her mother and Sarah to approach the two. "Mrs. Torgeson?"

Drawing near, she saw that Elaina's eyes were red and puffy; her face and arms were also cut and bruised. Glancing at Mrs. Torgeson, Caitlyn saw the same was true of her, only the mother's eyes were glazed in appearance, her face registering an element of shock and disbelief. She had no doubt in her mind that the Torgesons had had their own encounter with the storm, and the realization washed over her with increasing dread.

"We saw Andrew Foster as we were coming into town, and he told us we could find you here," Elaina said at last, her voice cracking with emotion. "M-mama and I... w-we thought you should know."

"What is it, Elaina?" Caitlyn asked, reaching for her hand. She squeezed the girl's fingers, hoping to offer some reassurance. But even so, Elaina's face crumpled. Caitlyn looked at Mrs. Torgeson over the girl's head, but the woman stared at her blankly, offering little in the way of explanation.

"It's James," Caitlyn heard Elaina say as she wiped away a tear. "H-he was in the barn, making sure all the animals were safe inside. We knew the storm was coming—we could see it from the house. I knew he was trying to hurry, but so many of the cows were outside. Th-there wasn't time. The cyclone took the barn first and then the house."

Elaina began to weep uncontrollably. Caitlyn pulled the girl close, and Elaina sobbed as the two clung to each other. "He's dead, Caitlyn. J-James is dead."

Sixteen

The room blurred before Caitlyn's eyes as she braced herself against Elaina's weeping form. She swayed to the side, her whole body beginning to tremble. The darkness overcame her, and she succumbed to its presence.

The next thing she knew, she was seated at one of the desks. Her mother knelt in front of her, grasping her hand, and she felt the gentle pressure of someone's hands on her shoulders. She slowly opened her eyes.

"Caitlyn," came her mother's gentle voice. "Are you all right?"

Caitlyn blinked a few times and looked around. Where was she? Why was everyone looking at her so strangely? And then it all came crashing back to her. Rena was gone and Matthew too. Now they were telling her James was dead. This couldn't be real. Would she ever break free of this nightmare?

In desperation, she attempted to stand. She had to escape it all! It was as if the walls of the schoolhouse were closing in on her, smothering her with a continual reminder of this awful reality.

"Easy," she heard Doc Ryberg say from behind her. "Just sit for a minute. Rest."

"W-what happened?" Caitlyn questioned, finding her voice. Her voice sounded so unlike her own; it quavered and shook on every word. She took a deep breath to try to calm herself. Her hands shook as she clasped them tightly in her lap.

"You fainted, dear," Mrs. Schmidt replied, taking her daughter's trembling hands once more and cradling them in her own.

"Oh, Miss Schmidt," Elaina said tearfully as she rushed to her side. "Are you all right?" The girl's tear-filled eyes emanated concern.

"I-I'm fine." Caitlyn knew she wasn't being honest, but what else could she say? Her thoughts barely registered the horrible truth: James was gone. Her head spun with the realization, and she gripped her mother's fingers in an effort to maintain her fragile sense of stability. She took a ragged breath, her shoulders shaking ever so slightly.

"You must have some breakfast," the doctor urged, his tone insistent. He gently pressed a warm biscuit into her hand. "It will make you feel stronger."

She stared at the food, suddenly too tired to even lift the offered biscuit to her lips. As if she were a child, her mother brought the biscuit forward in an effort to feed her. Caitlyn took a small bite, chewed, and swallowed, the nearly tasteless substance seeming to lodge in her throat. Someone placed a cup of coffee in her trembling hands, and she wound her fingers around its warmth.

In time, she felt she had garnered enough energy to stand. Doc Ryberg steadied her as she wavered.

"I must check on Madeline," she said, her voice no more than a whisper.

"Caitlyn, please..."

But her mother's plea faded into the distance as Caitlyn moved to Madeline's side. The child needed her and she wouldn't neglect her duty.

The rest of the day passed in a flurry of activity. Caitlyn resumed her role as nurse and caretaker, seeing to the injured and the needs of others. She ignored the concerned glances from her mother and Doc Ryberg. Sarah followed her like a shadow, assisting where needed and constantly asking Caitlyn about her health. Caitlyn disregarded the child's probing questions, throwing herself into the ever-mounting work. When the patients no longer required her full attention, she saw to the distribution of supplies outside the schoolhouse. As evening approached, she sat next to Madeline, coaxing the girl to drink the water she offered her. The little girl had yet to open her eyes, and she continued to complain of a headache. Caitlyn wished there were some way she could take the pain from the child. But she knew she

Beyond the Fury

could do nothing but keep her comfortable until her ailments began to diminish. She knew that very soon, Madeline's emotional pain would be far greater than her headache. As of yet, no one had told the child of her parents' deaths. Caitlyn was relieved, for at that moment, she could not find the words to express the horrible truth.

"Caitlyn, dear, please get some sleep." She felt her mother's hands on her shoulders, urging her away from Madeline. "You've been working hard all day."

"I'm fine, Mama," Caitlyn said softly, brushing her mother's concern aside.

"Look at me, Caitlyn," she said, stepping closer to her.

When Caitlyn didn't respond, she reached for her arm, turning her daughter to face her.

"Now I know you're hurting, but you need to be reasonable. I've told you before, you won't be of any help if you continue to wear yourself down like this."

Again Caitlyn didn't reply, and a moment later, Mrs. Schmidt turned away with a sigh. Caitlyn returned to Madeline's side.

The rain fell lightly outside as Caitlyn returned to the shelter of the schoolhouse. It had been raining all morning, a continuation of the persistent showers of the day before. It had been almost two days now since the storm, and Caitlyn continued to work among the injured. Madeline had revived somewhat, at last opening her eyes. She never questioned her surroundings, and for this, Caitlyn felt great relief. Caitlyn didn't think she would have the strength to answer the child's questions when the time came, especially when she didn't have the answers to her own whirling thoughts. She was exhausted, both physically and emotionally. She felt as if she had been walking through a haze, confused and disoriented. If it weren't for the pressing tasks that required her attention, she would probably collapse under the weight of it all.

Her mother had returned home earlier that morning, promising to come back to the school after she saw to a few things at the house. Caitlyn was surprised to see her father instead as he approached her from the other side of the room.

She hurried over to him, launching herself into his arms. She hadn't seen him since he had left her and Sarah at the schoolhouse, and she hadn't realized until that point just how much she had been longing to see him. He held her close for a long moment, his chin resting on the top of her head.

"Pa," she choked out, tears surfacing in her eyes. She hadn't cried since she and Andrew talked outside the previous morning, and she allowed herself the brief release.

"I know how difficult this must be for you," he said quietly, his deep voice full of concern. "Your ma has been worried about you."

Caitlyn nodded, but she didn't say anything. She laid her head on her father's shoulder and took a steadying breath.

"Your ma packed a bag for you," he told her, pointing to the sack he had placed on the floor. "There's some clothes and things in there for you and Madeline."

"Thank you," she said gratefully, thinking of how wonderful it would be to wear clean clothes again. Her dress was soiled with dirt and dried blood, and her apron had been torn to use for bandages.

"Andrew has been asking about you," her father told her. "He said he would stop by to see—"

"Miss Schmidt?"

Caitlyn whirled around to see Elaina Torgeson standing at the door. Her brother Joseph stood behind her, the rest of the family clustered around a horse-drawn wagon outside.

"It's time," the girl said tearfully. "We're going to the cemetery... for James."

Caitlyn understood the meaning behind her jumbled words. They were going to bury James. A sudden shiver wracked her body as she met the child's gaze.

"Pa wanted to know if you would like to come with us."

Caitlyn stole a glance at her father, reluctant to leave, but even more reluctant to venture outside the confines of the schoolhouse. She didn't want to accept the fact that James was gone. She didn't want to see the destruction. Most of all, she didn't want to go alone. True, the Torgesons would be with her, but they were lost in their own grief. She could hardly serve as the comfort they needed.

"Do you want to go, Caitlyn?" her father asked.

She wanted to say yes, but even so, conflicting thoughts rose to the surface. She forced herself to nod, instantly making the decision. She would be expected to mourn at James's gravesite, for she had been his intended. She must face reality; he was gone.

With her unspoken agreement, she joined Joseph and Elaina at the door.

"Do you want me to go with you, Cait?"

Her father's question brought relieved tears to her eyes. "Would you, Pa?"

He took the few steps to the door and drew an arm around her shoulders. The two followed the Torgeson children out into the rain, and they joined the procession to the cemetery. No one spoke along the way. Only the sound of muffled sobs greeted her ears. When they stood among the freshly dug graves, Caitlyn's father remained at her side, sheltering her somewhat from the rain. She leaned against him gratefully, thankful for his presence. At her other side stood Elaina. She slipped her hand in Caitlyn's, squeezing her fingers tightly. The measure of comfort was unspoken, but yet, meaningful.

The pastor spoke the customary funeral message and offered up a prayer. The service was brief, as there were other burials to conduct as well. At the conclusion of the service, Caitlyn stood behind with her father while the Torgesons paid their last respects. When the family turned from the grave, Elaina stepped close to Caitlyn and held out a single rose, the blossom remarkably untouched by the storm.

"For you," she said. "You can place it on his grave."

Caitlyn nodded as her vision blurred with tears. It seemed that tears would be a constant force with which she must always contend. She stepped forward, leaving her father's side. She knelt in front of the mound, her skirts settling around her. Mud seeped into the hem, but she paid little attention to the dampness. Her hand shook as she placed the rose over the earth that now covered the one she loved. She sat there for a long moment, her tears dampening the rain-soaked ground.

"I love you, James," she whispered brokenly. "I will always love you."

Seventeen

The sounds of hammering and men calling to one another echoed through the streets as Mr. Schmidt helped Caitlyn up into the wagon seat. He then lifted Madeline to sit next to her.

"Are you settled?" he asked as he rounded the wagon and then took up the reins.

Caitlyn nodded, unable to find her voice. The time had come to take Madeline home and away from the harsh conditions of the crowded schoolhouse. The child was still quite weak from her injuries, but every day she appeared to strengthen, a great encouragement to the family. Although Caitlyn continued to work at the schoolhouse organizing supplies and treating the injured, her parents had convinced her to return home for a few days. They wanted to get Madeline settled at home, and they hoped that Caitlyn could help the girl feel welcome.

As they moved through town, Caitlyn noted the rising structures and the clearing away of debris all around them. The telephone office and drugstore were under construction as well as the market. The signs of new development were everywhere: the scent of new lumber, the racket of hammers, and the sight of half-completed walls extending upward from newly constructed buildings. Caitlyn smiled slightly. It was good to see the progress being made, but even so, it was a constant reminder of the proceeding destruction, injury, and death.

In very little time, they reached the farm. Mr. Schmidt helped Caitlyn down from the wagon, and she held her arms out for Madeline. The girl clung tightly to her rag doll as she allowed Caitlyn to carry her to the house.

"There you are," Mrs. Schmidt called from the front porch.

Beyond the Fury

Caitlyn set Madeline down on the steps and turned toward her mother. "Hello, Mama," she said, knowing her smile was forced but yet not caring.

"Mama," Madeline said suddenly, now standing on the steps. "Where's my mama?"

Caitlyn froze, her gaze locked on the child. They had yet to tell the girl about her parents. What would they say? Would she understand?

"Where's my mama?" the girl repeated, enunciating each word with a stomp of her foot. "I want my mama!"

Mr. Schmidt approached the house from where he stood tending to the horses. He knelt down in front of the child, but his eyes wandered to Caitlyn.

Caitlyn shook her head, her eyes instantly pooling with tears. How could she possibly tell this child that her parents were dead? She had no desire to inflict further pain on her young life, but yet it looked like it was inevitable.

"No, you tell her," she whispered, turning toward the house. As much as she loved Madeline, there was no way she was going to watch her niece's life unravel in front of her. She couldn't bear the thought of the child's tears, her inconceivable loss. If only they didn't have to present her with such a horrible truth!

Caitlyn escaped into the dim confines of the house, surfacing tears obscuring the stairwell in front of her. She nearly tripped, but caught herself before she stumbled.

"Caitlyn..." came her mother's voice from the door.

Vaguely, Caitlyn heard her father's soothing words as he spoke to Madeline. "Come, darling, we're going to have a little talk."

"I want my mama!" the child wailed.

A sob escaped from Caitlyn as she scurried up the ladder to the loft. She flung herself across her bed, burying her face in the pillow. She tried to shut out the voices of her parents as they calmly spoke to Madeline, but it couldn't be done. Faintly, she heard her mother's gentle tone.

"Maddie, honey, your mama and papa—"

Tears welled in Caitlyn's eyes as she crushed the pillow down over her head, drowning out her father's explanations and her mother's words of comfort. Sobs shook her body as she waited for the dreaded reaction. And then her tears mingled with the piercing cries of the child, filling the tiny house with sudden intensity. *They must have told her,* Caitlyn thought, now cowering under the bedcovers. Part of her longed to comfort the girl, but she didn't think she would be able to witness Madeline's grief. There was so much she wanted to do for her, but she couldn't seem to summon the energy to rise from the bed either. She continued to hear Madeline's cries from the room below, her little body overcome with uncontrolled weeping, and Caitlyn couldn't prevent her own tears from overflowing and soaking her pillow.

    She must have fallen asleep, for when she opened her eyes and glanced around the room, everything was quiet except for the low murmur of voices from the parlor. It was dark, and light rain pattered against the roof and window. Caitlyn sat up slowly and rubbed a hand across her face. How long had she slept? *It couldn't have been long,* she reasoned. But then again, night had fallen and she couldn't recall what time it was when she had returned home with her father and Madeline.

    Madeline... How was the child? She instantly regretted her earlier neglect of her niece, and she rose from the bed quickly at the thought. She fumbled for the lamp that sat on the chest of drawers and lit the wick with trembling hands. She then ran a comb through her tangled hair and pinned it up in place. She knew she must look awful. She picked up her hand mirror, catching the glass's gleam in the lantern light. Though the room was dim, she could see herself clearly in the mirror. Her eyes were red and swollen, evidence of her earlier tears, and her face was completely devoid of expression. She fingered the wooden frame as a lonely tear trickled down her cheek. She brushed away the moisture, but that didn't prevent additional tears from spilling over. Caitlyn crushed the mirror against her chest, knowing that she couldn't possibly look at it any longer. It was too painful— her only reminder of James. Why did he have to go? Why had God taken him? They had been so in love, and in months they would have been married. Why had she been left to pick up the pieces— Madeline, the damaged structures, the destroyed homes and businesses, the injured?...

    Suddenly, the mirror flew from her hand, flung across the room with the force of her pent-up grief. She sank against the chest of drawers, gradually easing herself to the floor. She drew her knees up to her chest and buried her face in her skirt. She cried for a long while, bitter tears soaking into her calico dress. When at last her tears were spent, she rose to her feet, her legs shaky beneath her.

The mirror! What had she done with it? *It must be shattered into a million pieces,* she thought, another bout of tears overwhelming her. Certainly she had destroyed the only link to the one she loved! She frantically searched the dim room, terrified of what she would find. Expecting shards of glass and splintered wood, she was relieved to find the mirror intact. It had landed softly on the bed despite her careless treatment. She gathered the object into her hands, assessing its surface for any cracks or scratches. Finding no evidence of disrepair, she sighed with relief.

Caitlyn set the mirror on the chest of drawers next to the lantern, once more marveling at the detail contained in its surrounding frame. Then she extinguished the lantern, plunging the room into darkness. She took a few steps toward the edge of the loft, knowing she must see to Madeline. Draping a light shawl around her shoulders to alleviate some of the damp chill from the rain outside, Caitlyn approached the ladder. Slowly, she eased herself down into the kitchen. She took in her surroundings, noting the covered dish on the table. She lifted the lid, breathing in the delectable aroma of chicken soup. *How thoughtful of Mama to leave me supper,* Caitlyn thought as she retrieved a bowl and spoon from the cupboard. Then she set about making coffee. When she at last sat down to eat, she heard the hushed voices from the parlor again.

"I just don't know what to do," her mother was saying. "We're all dealing with our grief in our own way, but she…"

"How is she?" a familiar voice questioned, his tone full of concern. It only took Caitlyn a moment to identify the voice as belonging to Andrew.

They must be talking about Madeline, Caitlyn thought. Again, she wondered where the child was and how she had responded to word about her parents' absence.

"Completely unlike herself," her father replied. "She's really taking it hard. She cries, but yet there are times when I think she just tries to distract herself from the pain."

"With work," Andrew said. "But now that she's away from the schoolhouse, there will be less pressing matters."

Who were they talking about? They couldn't be referring to Madeline, could they? Why did they sound so concerned?

"She's been through so much," her mother continued. "If only..."

"It will take time," Andrew said, his voice quiet. "With Rena gone and..." His voice trailed off as well and the house was silent, but only for a moment.

"We're so sorry for your loss, Andrew," Caitlyn's mother said. "I'm sure you miss your brother a great deal."

"Thank you, Mrs. Schmidt." Even at a distance, Caitlyn could detect the suppressed emotion in his soft words. "Matthew and I... I guess we never thought it would come to something like this. After Ma and Pa passed away from the fever, we struck out on our own. We knew we had distant relatives in this area, so we came to start over. And now..."

Andrew would have to start over alone now, Caitlyn realized. He had no family left except for Madeline. Oh, how difficult this must be for him, and to think, she still had her ma and pa, which was more than Andrew could say. Perhaps he had come to take Madeline with him. After all, the child was just as close in relation to him as she was to Caitlyn. It seemed reasonable. But what would she do without Madeline— the only living legacy of her sister?

Caitlyn rose from her chair and cleared the table. She didn't know why, but she felt she must join them in the parlor. She approached the door apprehensively and tapped lightly on the wood paneling. Without waiting for a reply, she opened the door and stepped inside.

"Caitlyn," her mother said, rising from her chair.

Caitlyn motioned for her to resume her seat as she met her father's gaze.

"How are you feeling, Cait?" Her father's voice was gruff with emotion, and Caitlyn was surprised to see tears in his eyes.

"I'll be fine," she mumbled, her gaze traveling to Andrew who sat in the corner in her father's favorite chair. He held Madeline as she slept, and Caitlyn found herself touched at the tender sight.

"Hello, Caitlyn," he greeted, his eyes intent on hers. "Would you like to do the honors?" He stood, shifting the child in his arms as he walked toward her.

Beyond the Fury

"I-I don't understand," she said.

"I think it's time she went to bed," Andrew responded. "Even if she is sleeping already."

Caitlyn took the girl into her arms, her sleeping form emanating comforting warmth. "But I thought…"

"You thought what?" Andrew asked, clearly puzzled.

Caitlyn refused to meet his gaze. Instead, she fingered the lace collar on Madeline's nightgown.

"What is it, Caitlyn?" His voice was almost a whisper.

Caitlyn wasn't sure what compelled her to look up, but when she at last returned her gaze to his, Andrew looked at her with such tenderness, she could hardly hold the tears back.

"I thought you were going to take Madeline home with you," she mumbled, clutching the child closer.

Andrew shook his head. "Now why would I do that?" he said softly. "Anyone can see that she's perfectly content here. Besides, what home would I take her to— the boarding house? That's hardly a place for a child."

"But don't you want to care for her?" Caitlyn asked, instantly fearful of his reply.

"Permanently, you mean?" His query further prolonged the dreaded words she was sure would come.

Caitlyn only nodded.

"Oh, Caitlyn, there will be time for such talk later," he said softly. "Madeline will be fine here. You have taken good care of her… I thank you for that." He stepped closer and tentatively reached out a hand to brush a stray lock of hair away from her face. "I know you love her and will do everything you can to make her happy."

Caitlyn took comfort in his closeness and the seriousness of his words. She knew the matter wasn't settled, but for now, she could hold her niece and simply be thankful.

"I'm sorry," she whispered. "If only things could be different."

Andrew nodded, seeming to understand what was said, and yet, unsaid too. "Now, you get that child to bed," he commanded mildly.

"Yes, Sir," Caitlyn said with the slightest hint of a smile.

"Mama! Mama!"

Caitlyn startled awake at the sound of Madeline's cries. She sat up and reached for the screaming child, cradling her against her chest. "What is it, Maddie?" she murmured, rocking her back and forth. "Did you have a bad dream?"

The little girl squirmed in her arms, but Caitlyn held her tightly. Sobs shook her body with an intensity that frightened Caitlyn. What had upset her so greatly? If only she knew how to calm her!

"Maddie, honey, Auntie Caitlyn is here. Ssshhh, everything's going to be all right."

Caitlyn rose from the bed and began to pace the room, still holding the weeping child. She found herself humming softly, hoping to soothe her. A hymn tune from a recent church service came to mind, and over and over, she repeated the melody until Madeline relaxed against her. Caitlyn waited until she was certain that the girl was asleep, and then with careful gentleness, she laid Madeline on the mattress and tucked the covers securely around her. With an exhausted sigh, Caitlyn lay down beside her, drawing the girl close. In just a few minutes, Caitlyn also succumbed to the peacefulness of sleep.

Eighteen

Caitlyn left the loft early the next morning, rubbing the sleep from her eyes. Madeline still slept, and she had no desire to wake her. The tantalizing scents of frying pork and eggs greeted her as she entered the kitchen to find her mother hard at work at the stove. Her father sat at the table reading the paper, and to Caitlyn's surprise, Andrew sat next to him.

"Morning, Cait," Mr. Schmidt said quickly as he glanced up from his reading.

"Good morning, Pa... Andrew."

"Good morning," Andrew replied with a smile.

"Did you sleep well?" her father asked as Caitlyn relieved her mother of the heavy skillet she held. She carried it to the table and then sat across from Andrew.

"Not particularly," she said with a weak smile. "I think Maddie had a nightmare. I was probably up half the night with her."

"Why didn't you wake us?" Mrs. Schmidt asked as she joined them at the table. "Your pa or I could have sat with her."

"I'm surprised she didn't wake you with her screams," Caitlyn told them. "She was so scared. But it was no trouble, Mama, really. I eventually got her to sleep and she's fine now."

"Well, if it happens again, please call for us," her mother said.

Caitlyn nodded in consent as her father bent his head in the customary manner that alerted them that they would say a blessing over the food. But this morning, the prayer was not verbally spoken as was typical. When the supplication was complete, Mrs. Schmidt placed a spoon in the eggs and shoved the skillet toward Andrew.

"Eat up, Andrew," she said. "There's plenty."

Andrew dished up a hearty helping as instructed. "Thank you, Mrs. Schmidt... again."

"Oh, it's no trouble, Andrew. We're happy to have you," she said with a smile. At the puzzled look on Caitlyn's face, she explained, "Andrew has been coming every morning for breakfast ever since that first day after the storm. I guess we never told you."

Caitlyn moved the eggs around on her plate. "No, I guess not," she mumbled.

"I can see someone's not too happy that I'm here," Andrew teased, the familiar grin brightening his face.

Caitlyn felt the beginnings of a smile tug at her own lips. "I'm sorry, Andrew. I didn't mean to be so irritable," she apologized. "I'm just tired."

"Understandably so," he replied, his grin relaxing into mild concern. "Don't let Maddie wear you out now."

"I'll try not to," she said, raising a forkful of eggs to her mouth.

"Andrew's been working at Matthew and Rena's when he's not needed in town," Mrs. Schmidt told Caitlyn. "For the past few mornings, he's joined us for breakfast on his way out to the farm."

"Actually, I'll be heading out there this morning," Andrew said, laying down his fork. "Would you like to come with me, Caitlyn?"

"T-to Matthew and Rena's?" she asked in surprise. "But I couldn't—"

"I'll understand if you don't want to go," Andrew responded. "But I'm sure you or your mother would like to go through some of Rena's things."

"But I thought the tornado took the house," Caitlyn said, her breakfast quickly forgotten.

Andrew shook his head. "Both the house and barn are standing, but badly damaged. There's bound to be something you can salvage."

Caitlyn hadn't entertained the possibility up until this point. Could there really be something of Rena's left? She vaguely recalled Madeline's rag doll. Someone had retrieved 'Maddie doll' from the house, so there had to be more intact. A surge of hope welled up in her. As much as she hated the thought of the damage, she felt compelled to go and see for herself.

Beyond the Fury

"*Could* I go with you?" she asked eagerly.

"Sure. I'd be glad to have the company while I work," he responded. "Why don't we head out after breakfast then?"

"I can pack you two a lunch," Mrs. Schmidt suggested. "That way, you won't have to leave at noon."

"Thank you, Mrs. Schmidt. We'd appreciate that," Andrew replied.

As Mrs. Schmidt cleared away the breakfast dishes, Andrew picked up the paper and skimmed the front page. "I see quite a bit of funding has come in," he remarked. "It says here that Cumberland even donated their Fourth of July funds."

"That was generous of them," Caitlyn said as she wiped the table with a damp cloth.

"Yes, and other cities are sending more furniture, clothes, and food. Even people in Minnesota are making donations. I guess there'll be some work waiting for me in town in a few days. All of the supplies will need to be organized and distributed. Everything has been put on hold at the mill until repairs can be made, so I can afford to spend some time in town getting some things back in order."

"But we're not the only town needing assistance," Mr. Schmidt pointed out. "Clear Lake, Richardson, Clayton— they all reported damages. The storm's effects are everywhere."

Andrew continued to page through the paper, shaking his head when he came to the final page. He threw the paper down so suddenly that Caitlyn startled.

"What is it?" she asked, alarmed.

"A listing of those who died," he muttered. "I don't know why they have to publish that."

Caitlyn walked over to where he had left the paper and opened it to the last page. She scanned the list of names, knowing what she would find but yet dreading the truth. She traced her finger down the long columns, finding Matthew's name first. Close behind his listing was Rena's name. Much further down the list, she halted at the dreaded sight. It seemed so final— James Torgeson listed among the dead. There was no cause to doubt it, for she had seen it with her own eyes.

She folded the paper into its original state and turned away from the table. Surprisingly, she hadn't shed a tear, and for that she was grateful. As Delores Hamilton had said at the schoolhouse, there would be time for crying later. Now there was work to be done.

"Are you ready, Caitlyn?" Andrew asked as he turned toward the door.

She nodded and moved to stand at his side.

"I'll have her back some time this afternoon," Andrew told Mr. and Mrs. Schmidt.

"I hope Madeline will be all right with Mama today," Caitlyn said as Andrew helped her up into the wagon seat.

"I'm sure she will be fine," Andrew assured her. "Maybe she'll sleep awhile longer this morning. After last night, she needs the rest."

Caitlyn nodded. "I couldn't get her to sleep for the longest time. She cried and screamed... I didn't know how to help her. It seemed like everything I tried only made it worse. I sang to her, and that finally seemed to calm her a little... enough to get her to sleep."

Andrew reached for her hand and patted it gently. "You did everything you could for her," he said. "In time, she will come through this, just as we all will. She needs you... and I think you need her. We need to rely on each other now more than ever."

Tears stung at the back of her eyes as she realized what he said was true. In the midst of all the destruction and loss, the most important element existed in the people that had survived the storm. She lifted up a silent prayer of thanks for the lives that had been spared, especially of those she loved and cared for— her parents, Madeline, the Torgesons, her students, and Andrew. True, not everyone among those she loved had survived, but she knew she must also recognize this reality.

Caitlyn wasn't sure how long she was lost in her thoughts, but when she returned to the present, she noticed that Andrew still held her hand as he gripped the reins with the other. Sudden mortification washed over her when she glimpsed their interlocked fingers. She had buried her intended only days earlier, and there she was keeping company with another man and holding his hand too! If anyone saw her at that moment, her reputation would be marred for sure. She knew she should release her hand from his hold, but yet, she couldn't bring herself to remove her fingers from his reassuring grasp. She agonized over the

Beyond the Fury

matter for several moments, and then with determined resolve, she lifted her hand from beneath his and clasped her hands in her lap.

Neither spoke for the remainder of their brief journey, not even when they reached the Foster farm. Caitlyn could feel the awkward tension between them as Andrew helped her down from the wagon. He stepped away from her as soon as she stood securely on the ground. Wordlessly, he led the way toward the house and barn. The house stood next to the barn, damaged but still intact as Andrew had said. Part of the roof had been carried off, and several windows had blown in. Shingles and wood shavings were scattered over the ground, and a portion of a wall from the barn had been propped up against the house. Andrew made his way toward the barn, so Caitlyn felt free to venture to the house.

She entered by way of the back door, recalling times when she had come to visit her sister and her family. Inside the kitchen, Caitlyn's shoes crunched over broken glass and splintered furniture. As she approached the pantry cupboard, Caitlyn noted how the doors stood open at an awkward angle. A quick inspection told her that the hinges had been weakened. The small countertop was cluttered with dishes and cooking utensils that had fallen from their shelves. Caitlyn gasped as she recognized her mother's china, although most of it now consisted of fragments and pieces. Caitlyn's mother had given Rena the dishes the day she and Matthew were married, and now, almost the entire set was an utter loss. She bent to retrieve a chipped plate from the floor. Perhaps it could be salvaged.

She sorted through the remaining dishes, finding a few others damaged but still usable. Then she swept up the smashed remains and rid the room of additional debris. She didn't dare scrub the walls and floor clean, for the roof still gaped open over her head. Rain or dust could easily seep into the kitchen.

When she was satisfied with her work in the kitchen, she moved into the parlor, which had fared much better. Only a corner of the roof had leaked rain, and everything in that corner had been lost to water damage. Caitlyn looked about for any other signs of destruction, but what caught her eye was not evidence of the storm's wrath. Instead, she glimpsed the white taffeta draped over a chair, and she instantly knew it was her unfinished wedding dress. She recalled moving the gown into the parlor the day of the storm so they could eat the noon meal. She crossed to the chair and gathered the material into her arms. Oh, if only things could be different! Then Rena could help her finish the dress and she and James could plan their future together. When tears overcame her, Caitlyn did her best to hold her emotions inside. She would not cry over an unfinished wedding dress. She knew there were far more important things that required her attention.

"Did you want to eat dinner now?" came Andrew's voice from behind her. He stepped into the parlor as if he were afraid to intrude upon the quiet moment.

"Sure," she said, dashing at her tears before she turned toward him. "I'll get Mama's basket from the wagon."

"I already brought it into the kitchen," he replied, gesturing toward the other room. Caitlyn followed him into the kitchen where he had set the basket and jugs of water out on the table. The two sat down, bowing their heads in silent prayer. Then, before Andrew could serve himself, Caitlyn stood to uncover the food. She filled his plate with two sandwiches and a generous slice of her mother's apple pie.

"Thank you," he murmured as he accepted the offered food. When Caitlyn had served herself, Andrew picked up his sandwich as if to eat, but seconds later, he set the food down again. He looked at her across the table, seriousness etched in his blue eyes.

"That was your wedding dress you found, wasn't it?" he asked, his voice soft.

Caitlyn nodded, her gaze falling to the sandwich in front of her.

"I'm sorry," he mumbled. "That must have been hard for you."

She nodded again, still avoiding his eyes.

"I'm sorry too... about James."

It was the first time since the storm that he had spoken of her intended by name, and Caitlyn looked up at him in surprise. The sympathy she saw in his eyes melted the earlier tension between them, and she felt unexpected tears pool in her eyes.

"I'm sorry," she whispered in return. "You must miss Matthew." She had not expressed her sympathies verbally to Andrew, and now that they had each made reference to the other's emotional pain, it was as if a wall had crumbled between them.

Andrew stood and moved to her side of the table, taking both her hands in his. He gazed at her for a long time, and Caitlyn returned his unwavering attentiveness. She saw the pain reflected in his expressive eyes, and she wished she could rid him of everything he had experienced since the storm. But it was not to be. There was nothing that would erase the heartache.

Caitlyn felt the gentle pressure of Andrew's hands as they continued to clasp her own. Once more, she released herself from his hold and returned her attention to her lunch. The remainder of the meal was completed in silence.

When Caitlyn returned home later that afternoon, she carried a crate filled with some of Rena and Madeline's clothes, bolts of cloth, serviceable dishes, bedding, and her wedding dress. Andrew carried Rena's hope chest into the parlor where Caitlyn could sort through its contents later. Mrs. Schmidt invited Andrew to stay for supper, but he declined, saying he needed to see to a few things in town. Caitlyn breathed an inward sigh of relief, the preceding afternoon at the center of her thoughts. She knew that the days of cheerful banter between her and Andrew had disappeared along with their earlier friendship. Nothing would ever be the same between them again.

Nineteen

The hot July wind swept over the parched ground as Caitlyn struggled with the heavy bucket, brimming with fresh water from the well. She carried the bucket toward the house, stopping every few minutes to rest due to the strain of her heavy burden. She was careful not to let too much water slosh over the sides, but even so, she felt the cool wetness trickle over her bare feet every so often. Once inside the house, she leaned against the closed door to rest. She wiped the sweat from her forehead with a corner of her apron, wishing the gathering clouds outside would bring the rain they so desperately needed. But just as soon as the thought entered her head, she shoved it aside. The last time she had prayed for a cooling shower, the threatening skies had dropped a tornado.

"Caitlyn, can you bring the water into the kitchen?" Mrs. Schmidt asked. "I need to be getting some supper around."

"Yes, Mama. I'm coming."

Caitlyn carried the bucket into the kitchen as directed, sighing heavily when she set it by the stove. "What do you plan to make for supper?"

"Oh, nothing fancy," her mother replied. "It's too hot to think about cooking anything. I brought in some things from the garden, and maybe we can make up a few sandwiches."

"Do you need any help?" Caitlyn asked.

"Oh, not just yet, but you could check on Madeline. She's playing out back on that swing your pa made for her."

Caitlyn nodded and reached for a cup that sat on the table. She dipped the cup in the bucket of water and took a long drink. After she had refreshed herself, she turned once more to go outside. She found Madeline behind the house, struggling to make the little swing propel itself forward. Caitlyn smiled as she witnessed the girl's determination. She tried to create momentum, but her legs were too short to push the swing to the desired height.

"Auntie Caitlyn!" the child cried when she saw her. "Help me swing!"

Caitlyn grinned as she ran toward her niece. She took hold of the swing from behind, gently prodding it upward and forward. When the girl and swing fell back into her hands, she repeated the action again, over and over.

"More! Higher!" Madeline cried, her giggles filling the stifling, late afternoon air. Caitlyn continued to push the swing, gradually feeling the initial energy leave her arms.

"But Auntie Caitlyn's tired," she objected after awhile.

The words were barely out of her mouth when she saw Andrew making his way toward them from the barn. She had forgotten he came to help her father with the chores every so often.

"Mind if I take over for awhile?" he asked Caitlyn when he reached them.

She stepped away from Madeline with a smile. "She's all yours," she said.

As Caitlyn moved a distance away to better observe their playful interaction, she couldn't help but feel as if she were walking away from Madeline permanently. Andrew had come to play with Madeline several times over the past few weeks, and each time, Caitlyn felt as if she were an intruder. It was clear Andrew loved the child. Caitlyn had no doubt he would see to the girl's needs if given the opportunity, but he had never vocalized the possibility of taking Madeline with him. He had said they would discuss the matter at a later date, but they had yet to speak of Madeline's future. Caitlyn knew he could initiate that conversation at any time, and every day, she prepared herself for the inevitable. Andrew would assume the role of Madeline's guardian, and although she longed to care for the child herself, she would let him see to the task instead. Andrew deserved to take the girl into his home. He had no one left that he could consider immediate family. Madeline was his only link to Matthew and his earlier deceased parents. He and Madeline had every right to begin a life of their own.

"Supper's ready," Mrs. Schmidt called from the open kitchen window. And with those words, Caitlyn, Andrew, and Madeline joined her parents inside for the evening meal.

"Is she asleep?" Mrs. Schmidt asked as Caitlyn entered the kitchen. The supper dishes had been cleared away, and her mother had set a pot of tea and a plate of sugar cookies on the table.

Caitlyn nodded. "For now," she said. "There's no telling when she'll wake up after another nightmare."

"Poor child," Mrs. Schmidt said with a sigh. "She's been through so much. It's so wonderful to see her happy. She really enjoys that swing, and when Andrew's here, it's like her whole world brightens."

"She loves him," Caitlyn replied. "Anyone can see that."

"Well, he's certainly been coming around often," her mother said, pulling out a chair so she could sit down at the table. "Will you join me for a cup of tea?"

Caitlyn sat down next to her mother and reached for the teapot. She poured a cup for her mother and then one for herself. "He wants to spend time with Maddie," Caitlyn said in reference to her mother's earlier comment.

"But it seems to me that there's more to his visits than he lets on," she said as she took a cookie and bit into it.

"What do you mean?"

"Well, he wouldn't come almost every day just to see Madeline, would he?"

"Why not?" Caitlyn questioned. "He loves Maddie just as much as we do."

"Caitlyn, surely you haven't missed the way he looks at you," her mother said. "It's obvious he cares for you, and I think he always has... ever since Rena and Matthew brought our families together."

"But Mama, it's not like that with Andrew and me," Caitlyn objected. "We're only friends. And besides, even if Andrew is interested in me, which I'm sure he isn't, I couldn't be seen with him. It's much too soon; it wouldn't be proper."

Beyond the Fury

"Perhaps not," her mother agreed. "But I'm only telling you what I've seen, and I really feel his visits have been with you in mind as well as Madeline."

"He has implied no such thing," Caitlyn responded. "Please Mama, don't say anything more."

"I'm sorry if I've upset you, dear," she said with an apologetic smile. She reached out to touch her daughter's arm, gazing at her intently for a moment. "But there's something else bothering you. Am I right?"

Caitlyn stared down at the dark liquid in her teacup, avoiding her mother's eyes. *How did she always seem to sense when something was wrong?* There was no hiding from her mother's perceptiveness.

"It's nothing, Mama," she mumbled. "I'm just worried about Maddie, that's all."

"How so?" her mother asked, her face registering concern.

Caitlyn lifted her teacup to her lips and sipped her tea slowly. "Well, not Maddie exactly," she admitted, her gaze traveling to the tablecloth. "Maybe I'm just being selfish."

"I don't understand," Mrs. Schmidt said. "What's got you so worried?"

Caitlyn met her mother's eyes and sighed. "I want Madeline to stay with us, to be a part of our family, but…"

Mrs. Schmidt waited while Caitlyn tried to formulate her words.

"But I think Andrew wants the same for him, and I'm afraid he'll want to raise Madeline," she finally said, her voice trembling.

"Has he said anything that leads you to believe he wants to care for her?" her mother asked.

"Well, not really, but I know he loves her. I can see it in his eyes; he wants Madeline for himself. He said we'd talk about it soon, but he hasn't said anything since."

"I think that was his way of skirting the matter at the time, Caitlyn. Andrew can see that you're perfectly capable of caring for Madeline. The child has faced so much change already. If he were to take her home to the boardinghouse, it would be another adjustment for her, and we all know that she's not ready for that."

Caitlyn nodded. "But he's her uncle. Don't you think he deserves to be a part of her life?"

"He is, Caitlyn," her mother objected. "He's here almost every day to see her."

"But what if he wants more?"

"Then he'll tell us," her mother replied, leaving no room for argument. "Really, I don't think you have anything to worry about. Right now, we need to make sure that Madeline receives the care she needs. The rest will work itself out in time." She patted her daughter's hand with a reassuring smile. "I think it's time we get some sleep. Morning will come before we know it."

Twenty

"Oh, here's your pa with the mail," Mrs. Schmidt announced the next afternoon. "And it looks like there's quite a bit of it."

Caitlyn's father jumped from the wagon and began to unhitch the horses. "There's a letter for you, Emily," Pa said as Caitlyn and her mother joined him outside. He sorted through the stack of envelopes until he found the one he had been seeking. "Here it is... from Minneapolis."

"It's from Uncle Richard and Aunt Laura," Mrs. Schmidt said as she examined the envelope. "I wonder what this is all about." She tore open the flap and extracted a single sheet of paper. She read silently for a few minutes and then looked to her daughter. "Your cousin Maggie is getting married, and we have been invited to the ceremony... your pa and I," she said.

"That's wonderful," Caitlyn exclaimed. "So will the wedding be in Minneapolis?"

"Yes, on the fifth of August. We'll have to send our regards though since we won't be able to attend."

"But why?" Caitlyn wanted to know. "You should go, Mama. It's not every day your niece gets married. I'm sure it will be a fine wedding since it will be in the city. Besides, you haven't seen Uncle Richard and Aunt Laura for years."

"Yes, it would be wonderful to go," Mrs. Schmidt admitted. "But there's so much to do here. They need all the help they can get in town, and then there's Madeline..."

"I'll see to Madeline while you're gone," Caitlyn told her. "And August fifth is weeks away yet. You might be able to set aside some time by then. Don't pass up this opportunity until you know for sure; think about it for awhile."

Her parents exchanged glances. "We'll consider it," her father said. "But why do you want us to go so badly? You're so quick to be rid of us."

"Of course not," Caitlyn said with a laugh. She suddenly realized it had been her first real laugh in a long time, and she could honestly say it felt good.

"Then what is it?" her father pressed.

Caitlyn looked at them with seriousness. "I just think you deserve a day away," she said. "You've been working so hard, and it's time you have a day to yourselves."

"That's sweet of you, Caitlyn," her mother said, resting a hand on her shoulder. "We'll talk about it later, closer to the date. But for now, why don't we make some lemonade? I'm sure your father could use something cool after his trip into town."

"You've got that right," her father said with a grin as he turned to lead the horses to the barn. "It'll be just the thing to cool me off before I do the chores."

"What about Andrew?" Caitlyn asked. "I'm sure he'd like a little lemonade."

"He won't be helping today," her father called over his shoulder. "He said something about working at Matthew and Rena's house. He wanted to get the roof in good shape before it rains again. The place has enough water damage as it is."

Caitlyn turned toward her mother. "He's got to be miserable out there. With weather like this, the roof would be the last place I'd choose to be if I were him."

"Yes, but it needs to be done," Mrs. Schmidt countered. "Perhaps you'd like to bring him some refreshment."

"Me? Now?"

"Well, why not? I know concern when I see it."

"But Mama—"

"Here, I'll mix up a jug of lemonade and you can take it to him," her mother interjected. "Besides, I think he would enjoy a visit from you." Caitlyn didn't miss the twinkle in her mother's eye.

"But—"

Mrs. Schmidt shook her head. "That boy has been working so hard. The least you can do is bring him a cool drink on a hot day."

"All right, Mama, I'll go. But there's nothing more to this than just a glass of lemonade. Please refrain from any further matchmaking."

"I've done nothing of the sort," she said with a smile. Then, almost immediately, her mirth faded. "I'm sorry, Caitlyn.

Beyond the Fury

I know that you're still grieving for James. Please don't think that I'm pressing you to abandon any love you may have in your heart for him."

Caitlyn turned away, not wanting to see the sympathy she was sure emanated from her mother's eyes. *Why did she have to go and say that?* her thoughts screamed. As if every waking moment didn't remind her of the fact: James was gone, and Matthew and Rena... *Oh, why had everything come to this?*

"I'm sorry, Caitlyn," her mother's voice came again, thick with tears. "I didn't mean—"

"I'm fine, Mama," she mumbled, reaching for the lemonade pitcher. Without another word, she capped the jug after filling it with the liquid, and then turned toward the door. "Don't keep supper waiting for me. I'm not hungry anyway."

She didn't give her mother time to reply as the door closed behind her. Outside, the hot wind tossed a few errant strands of hair in front of her face, and she brushed them back into place with her free hand. But her attempts were futile. She ignored her stubborn hair as she placed the jug of lemonade in the saddlebag and mounted the horse. She tried to clear her head as the mare trotted forward. Her mother hadn't intended to upset her with the things she said, but the truth was, she had. There was no avoiding the obvious: she couldn't rid herself of the ever-present loss and longing. Would she ever be able to release herself from the oppressive hold?

She kept her gaze forward on the road ahead, striving to banish the force of her emotions. Dark clouds had gathered on the horizon, and she hoped the possibility of rain would present her with the necessity to deliver the lemonade and be on her way. She couldn't let Andrew see her like this. She must free herself of thoughts of James and the others lost in the storm. If she dwelt on such matters any longer, she wouldn't be fit for general conversation, let alone friendly company.

Upon reaching the farm, she caught sight of Andrew as he climbed down the ladder from the roof.

"Why, Caitlyn," he exclaimed. "What brings you out here?" He wiped sweat from his forehead with a rag he had pulled from his pocket.

"I brought you some lemonade," she said, dismounting before he could offer to assist her. "I thought you might be thirsty." She knew her smile was strained, and she vowed to continue this forced action.

"Thank you," he said, accepting the jug from her outstretched hand. "You'll join me inside, won't you? I'd really appreciate the company."

"I'm afraid I wouldn't be good company at all," she mumbled, turning back to the saddled horse.

"Let me be the judge of that," he said, reaching for her hand. "Please come inside for a few minutes before you head back. I haven't seen anyone all day, and it would be nice to rest for awhile."

Caitlyn contemplated for a moment before responding. "All right," she said, somewhat reluctantly. "But only for a little while."

A distant rumble of thunder disturbed the quiet countryside, and Andrew glanced toward the west as lightning slashed across the darkening sky.

"Well, we'd best get inside before it rains."

Caitlyn allowed him to lead her inside. When the door closed behind them, the two moved into the kitchen. Caitlyn set the jug of lemonade on the table as Andrew pulled out a chair and indicated that she should be seated. He retrieved two cups from the cupboard and poured some lemonade into both of them. When he took the seat across from her, he placed one of the glasses before her.

"I'm sorry I didn't bring any cookies or something else to eat," she apologized.

"This is fine," he said with a smile. He took a sip of his lemonade and the room fell into silence. Rain pattered on the newly repaired roof above them while thunder continued to rumble in the distance. A bright flash of lightning caught Caitlyn by surprise, and she uttered a startled sound that earned a laugh from Andrew.

"It's just lightning," he said with a chuckle.

"I know," she replied. "It's just... ever since, I get a little nervous when storms come up."

"I know what you mean," he said softly. "But this is just your average thunderstorm. Nothing more will come of it."

Beyond the Fury

"But tornadoes can strike anywhere," Caitlyn pointed out. "I think we all know that from experience now."

"A tornado never strikes the same place twice," he said, gesturing toward the window. "It's kind of like lightning. How many times have you heard of lightning striking anywhere more than once?"

"I know, but I don't think I'll ever have the same view of a thunderstorm again."

Andrew nodded in understanding, and once more, silence reigned in the kitchen. Caitlyn offered up a silent prayer of thanks, grateful that Andrew had finished his work on the roof. If not for the repairs, they would have been drenched with rainwater. She shivered at the thought, and rose to pace the room, hoping to ward off the sudden chill.

"Are you cold?" Andrew asked, also rising to his feet. "The rain has cooled things off quite a bit. I could build us a fire."

"No," Caitlyn said quickly. "I'm fine." She returned to the table and bunched her hands in her lap. Maybe the room *was* a little chilly, but she wouldn't admit it. She wanted to go home. She had come to deliver the lemonade— not to stay and linger over the refreshment with him. It wasn't that she didn't enjoy his company; she just simply wanted to be alone where she could sort out her conflicting thoughts. And the longer she stayed in the house with him, the more opportunity he had to bring up Madeline and the matter of her guardianship. She had to go.

"I really should be going," she vocalized.

Andrew shook his head. "Not in this rain. You'll be soaked through to the skin. At least wait until the storm passes."

Reluctantly, she nodded. Andrew set aside his lemonade and disappeared into the parlor. Caitlyn couldn't refrain from tidying the kitchen, even if there was hardly anything to clean. The room still showed the results of her earlier efforts. Only a few water-soaked areas required her attention. She had just set the cleaning rag aside when she heard Andrew call to her from the parlor.

"Caitlyn, come in here where it's warm," he invited.

Caitlyn shivered again, the kitchen offering little warmth. *A short time in front of the fire won't hurt anything,* she reasoned. As soon as the rain let up, she would head home.

She entered the parlor, immediately taking notice of the fire that he had lit in the fireplace. The warmth of the flames drew her forward until she stood in front of their glow. She warmed herself for a moment, listening to the rain as it clattered against the roof overhead.

"I'm glad you were able to fix the roof before the storm hit," she finally said aloud. "If you hadn't, then lighting a fire would have been impossible."

He laughed lightly, and Caitlyn took delight in the welcome sound. "Come sit by me," he said, a smile in his voice. "I want to hear how Madeline has been over the past few days." He patted the couch cushion next to him, and despite her reluctance to remain in his presence, she sat down beside him.

"Madeline's fine," she replied. "But she misses you. You must have been busy lately."

"Yes, I've been here working on the house."

"What do you intend to do with it when everything is back in order?"

As soon as she uttered the question, she regretted it. How could she have been so careless in initiating the dreaded conversation? The answer was obvious: he wanted Matthew's house so he could have a proper place to raise Madeline.

"Well, I thought I could live here," Andrew said, breaking into her thoughts. "That is, if you don't mind."

"Why would I mind if you lived here?" Caitlyn asked, dreading his reply.

"Well, it was your sister's house... Matthew built it for her. I thought maybe you would feel as if I were intruding on memories of your family."

Caitlyn shook her head, relief filling her. "Matthew was your brother," she practically whispered. "He would have wanted you to have the house."

"That's what I've thought too," he said just as softly. "But Caitlyn... if there's anything you'd like of Rena's... anything, just ask."

Caitlyn shook her head. "I have everything I want," she said. "The rest is yours." *Except Madeline,* she silently added.

"So Madeline is all right then?"

Andrew's reference to the child jolted her from her similar thoughts.

"Yes, except for the nightmares," she replied.

"Still?" Andrew exclaimed softly. "I thought you said she hadn't had one in a few weeks."

"Last night she had another," she said. "She screamed and cried for nearly an hour until I could get her to sleep again. I felt so helpless. Nothing I did seemed to make any difference."

Caitlyn caught the pained expression that passed over Andrew's face, and she immediately felt that she had disappointed him with her lack of skill in caring for Madeline.

"You must think me completely inadequate," she whispered, horrified that tears were brimming in her eyes. She turned her gaze toward the fire, unable to bear the thought that she had failed in this way.

She felt his hand on her shoulder as he angled himself on the couch so he could better see her face. "Cait," he said softly. "How could you think that?"

Caitlyn's breath left her at his shortened use of her name, usually only spoken among family. His gentle tone drew her gaze back to his, and his face blurred before her as her eyes misted with held-in tears.

"Madeline deserves so much more," she said brokenly as she brushed the tears away with the back of her hand. "I can't take away the nightmares; I don't even know what to say to her. I couldn't even tell her that Rena and Matthew had died. I left, Andrew. I couldn't even stay in the room when Ma and Pa told her. I should have been there when she needed me most, but I walked away. I should have been with her when the storm hit. Then maybe Matthew or Rena would have made it out alive. But no, I went home with Ma and Pa and left them... and you. I should have done something. I could have—"

Andrew placed both hands on her upper arms. "Caitlyn, there's nothing you could have done, even if you had been right there next to them. It was time for them to go, and God was calling them home. He placed you at a distance so you could help others. He wanted you to carry on with your life, caring for Madeline and your family. He has a purpose for you, Caitlyn."

"But things could have been different. If Ma and Pa hadn't come along when they did, I would have stayed in the wagon with Rena and Madeline. Maybe I could have helped with Madeline in the dry-goods store. Maybe—"

"You could have lost your own life."

The truth of Andrew's words cut through her ramblings, and she let out a ragged sigh. "But I should have been there," she whispered, her voice catching on resurfacing tears.

Andrew shook his head. "I'm thankful you were safe at home. You will never know the nightmare that came through town. It was like a monster, Caitlyn… thick and black. I can't even begin to explain the sound; it was like continuous thunder, thousands of cannons or guns, a train racing down the tracks with such speed, there was no stopping it. There was no warning— only the dead quiet before it hit.

"I was in the general store, standing by the counter. Reverend Adams ran in and yelled something about a cyclone coming, but there wasn't enough time. By the time I got to the stairs above the cellar, everything was still. The air was so thick I could hardly breathe, and then suddenly, everything started falling. I could only stand there in the stairwell and wait for it to pass. There was nothing else I could do. I could feel the debris coming down on top of me, and I had to keep myself from being buried underneath it all. I could hear everyone screaming down below, but I couldn't help them… not until it was over. And even then, I had to wait for someone to pull me out. I did everything I could to help get everyone out of the cellar, but for some, it was too late. That's when I knew I had to find all of you. I had no idea you had gone home with your parents, so when I didn't find you with Rena, Matthew, and Madeline, I thought for sure you were gone. I thought we would never find you… alive that is. But when I saw you at the schoolhouse…"

Andrew's eyes filled with tears and his voice shook. "God saved you from having to endure the storm. He protected you, and I've thanked Him every day since. I don't know what Madeline would do without you… *I* don't know what I would do without you.

"If not for you and your parents, Maddie would be living with me at the boardinghouse. I wouldn't have the

Beyond the Fury

slightest idea as to how to care for her, but you seem to know exactly what to do. Why, you won't even leave her without some instruction as to what to feed her or how to dress her. And you're continually worrying about how she'll get along when you're not around. You're attentive to her every need. There's no one better suited to care for her than you. It's obvious that you're doing the best you can."

"But how can I be offering her my very best when there's so much I don't know? I'm not ready to raise a child."

"You're not alone in this, Caitlyn. Your ma and pa are there to help, and I'll do everything I can to make things easier for you." He reached for her hand and squeezed it gently. "You don't have to do all of this on your own. Lean on the Lord for strength; let others help you."

As much as Caitlyn wanted to take comfort in his words, she couldn't face the possibility of relinquishing Madeline's care to anyone else, even if it would only be for a short time.

"I can't," she said, rising from the couch and pacing the room. "I won't leave her."

"No one's asking you to," he replied as he moved to stand in front of her. "And no one will take her away from you."

"Not even you?"

Twenty-one

She had spoken without thinking, and now there was no turning back. Andrew stared at her; his sky blue eyes widened in the flickering firelight.

"What are you talking about, Caitlyn?" he asked, reaching his hand out to her. But she turned away from him, sudden tears rising in her eyes. "You couldn't possibly think that I'd—"

"You have every right to claim Madeline as your own. She *is* your niece after all."

"But I don't understand…" Andrew faltered. "She's your niece too. Why would I deprive you of Rena's child? How could you even think I would do that to you? You love Maddie, and she returns your love."

"But you love her too," Caitlyn objected.

"Of course I do," he said, his voice husky with emotion. "But allowing you to care for her doesn't mean I love her any less. You can give her so much more than I could ever hope to dream. She needs you, Caitlyn."

Tears spilled from her eyes unheeded, and she took another step backward. This time, Andrew caught her hand and drew her close to him.

"I won't lie to you; I would love nothing more than to offer Madeline a full and happy life," he said. "But I can't do that on my own. I truly believe God has appointed you to that task."

He was offering her the most precious gift of all—guardianship of Madeline— and suddenly, she couldn't seem to accept it. He deserved to share in the child's growth and development too. She wouldn't allow him to abandon that privilege.

"She adores you," Caitlyn told him. "And she looks up to you. How can you just leave her to me, no questions asked?"

"I'm not going anywhere," he practically whispered. "I could never leave her. But I want what's best for her… and it's you, Caitlyn."

Caitlyn gazed at him intently, her tears now gone. He met her eyes, unwavering in his gaze. "You won't leave then?" she whispered.

"Where would I go? This is my home." His words left no room for debate.

"But I thought that with Matthew gone—"

"That there would be nothing left for me here?" he finished. "You couldn't be more wrong, Caitlyn. Everything I care about is right here in New Richmond; I consider your family to be my family."

"I'm glad you feel that way," she said, her voice sounding small and timid in the spacious parlor. "You've always been a part of our family, and nothing will change that. Matthew may not be here, but that doesn't mean you can't be a part of our lives."

"You don't know how much it means to me to hear you say that," he said softly. He pulled her close, and she rested her head against his shoulder. She knew she should move away from him, but even so, she let him hold her. She couldn't deny the contentment she found in his arms, even though she was aware that it wasn't proper; James had only been gone for a few weeks. But she told herself that she had accepted Andrew's embrace simply as a means of comfort. They were both experiencing the same feelings of loss, confusion, and helplessness… She needed to be close to him. She felt powerless to free herself from the arms that held her so gently.

They stood there for only minutes, but to Caitlyn, it seemed like forever. When he released her, she felt an overwhelming emptiness wash over her. She touched his arm, silently pleading for his closeness, but he stepped away from her, retreating toward the couch.

"It stopped raining," he said, his voice rough with some undefined emotion. "Maybe you should be heading back home."

Caitlyn felt the rejection even before he spoke. She avoided his eyes, the distance between them revealing a tension so powerful, she didn't know how to react. She found herself moving toward the door, her feet seeming to have a will of their own, but her heart pleading with her to stay. She said nothing as she opened the door. She didn't even glance behind her, although she hoped he would call her back to his side. With tears brimming in her eyes, she closed the door softly behind her, a sense of utter helplessness beginning to weaken her resolve. She almost turned back to the door, but she bit her lip against the inner pain and pressed forward.

Caitlyn sat down on the edge of the bed, looking down on Madeline's sleeping form in the flickering candlelight. Her earlier conversation with Andrew came back to her, and she was immediately thankful that the child still remained with her. She knew Andrew to be a fine man of character, but even so, she had entertained the thought that he could whisk Madeline away without so much as an explanation. He loved the child greatly, and Caitlyn could tell that being a visitor in their home just so he could see the girl was extremely difficult for him. If only there was something she could do to remedy the situation. She knew she must appear selfish to Andrew, clinging to Madeline as if she laid some claim to her. But the truth was, Caitlyn felt it was her duty to care for the child as if she were her own. Although she knew her parents or Andrew could do the same, she had already grown to accept Madeline as a part of her future. She and Andrew hadn't reached any conclusions in their earlier conversation, even though it appeared that he had completely resigned Madeline to her care. Even so, Caitlyn found she didn't feel right about it. Andrew had seemed content with the arrangement, but there was no mistaking the deep sadness in his eyes.

There had to be some way to alleviate the emotional strain on both sides— for him and her. They were each in equal position to accept responsibility for Madeline, and although Caitlyn had obtained the guardianship she so desperately wanted, she felt again with distinct certainty that she couldn't do it on her own. Andrew had admitted the same, and she had readily understood. But now Caitlyn had to face the truth; she couldn't raise the child on her own either. She needed the help of others and the Lord's guidance to direct her, just as Andrew had said.

She slipped from the bed and knelt on the floor beside the mattress. "Oh, God," she whispered into the semi-darkness. "Please help me to know what to do. Please direct my thoughts and plans in the way You would want them to unfold. Bless all those I love, and may we all look to You and each other in everything we do. I pray You would comfort Madeline tonight as she sleeps. Let her sleep peacefully... without any nightmares. And God, comfort Andrew in Your own special way. He needs Your love now more than ever. I ask all of this in Your precious name, Jesus. Amen."

Caitlyn slipped under the covers next to Madeline and cuddled the girl close. She closed her eyes and let the peacefulness of sleep come over her. In the morning, she would consider what lay ahead.

Twenty-two

"Andrew's coming for supper," Mrs. Schmidt said a few evenings later. "So you'll need to set an extra place at the table."

Caitlyn nodded and turned to Madeline who was playing on the floor. "Maddie, honey, why don't you help me set the table. Uncle Andrew is coming to visit."

The child's eyes lit up with excitement at the mention of Andrew's name, and Caitlyn felt a brief moment of jealousy. If the roles were reversed and Madeline lived with Andrew, would Madeline be as excited to see her? Caitlyn did her best to shove the thought aside. She didn't want to dwell on such matters mere moments before Andrew would enter the house. He had been helping her father with chores that afternoon, and according to the clock, the men would be inside shortly.

"Caitlyn, is everything all right?" Mrs. Schmidt asked as she handed Madeline a plate and cup. The girl loved to set the table, and her wide smile and bright eyes told Caitlyn she was proud to help in this way.

"Yes, Mama. I'm fine," Caitlyn replied as she checked on the stew bubbling on the stove.

"You seem out of sorts. Are you sure you're feeling all right?"

Caitlyn nodded. "I guess I was just thinking," she said absent-mindedly as she watched Madeline place a fork by each plate.

"About Madeline?" Mrs. Schmidt responded, her gaze resting briefly on the little girl.

Caitlyn couldn't deny her mother's assumption, for it was true. It seemed the child was at the center of her thoughts at every moment.

"You're still worried that he'll want to take care of her, aren't you? But I thought you and Andrew discussed it."

"We did," Caitlyn admitted. "But…"

"Why can't you believe him when he says he loves Maddie, but he wants you to raise her? He truly feels she would be better off with you."

"But it isn't right," Caitlyn objected. "I can see the love in his eyes when he looks at her. He deserves so much more. Madeline is the only family he has left, Mama. This arrangement isn't fair to Andrew, and it isn't fair to Madeline."

"But what about you, Caitlyn? What do you want?"

Caitlyn's eyes filled with tears as she glanced at Madeline, willing to keep her emotions in check. "I want to raise Madeline as my own," she practically whispered. "But I need to consider all of this beyond myself, ignoring my selfish wants. What's best for Madeline may not be what I want."

"Are you saying you think Andrew should care for her?" her mother asked, her eyes widening in surprise.

"No, not necessarily," Caitlyn whispered. "I just wish there were an easier way to work through all of this. Rena and Matthew wouldn't have wanted this for Madeline. She needs a home… a permanent home with those she loves. I can't care for her on my own; Andrew doesn't think he can either. Maybe you and Pa could—"

"My does it smell good in here," Andrew exclaimed as he entered the kitchen.

Caitlyn turned toward him, wondering how much he had overheard. But he gave no indication that he was aware of their conversation as he scooped Madeline into his arms and swung her around in circles.

"How's my girl?" he asked amid the child's giggles.

Caitlyn moved toward the stove, intending to busy herself with the stew and bread. She heard Madeline's reply, but only vaguely. She couldn't bear to witness their playful interaction, even though she longed to be a part of it. She set the food on the table, all the while avoiding her mother's gaze and the pair laughing and talking by the parlor door. When her father joined them for the meal, Caitlyn kept her eyes on her plate.

Her mind began to wander to their visitor. It seemed that every time she turned around, Andrew was there: joining them for supper, playing with Madeline, standing by whenever Caitlyn needed him. Her thoughts traveled back to their brief embrace in the Fosters' parlor. There was no denying the security she felt as he held her close. There was also no denying that Madeline had drawn them together since the storm. She was a child in need of care and nurturing who depended on both of them. Where at one time Andrew had melted into the background, a casual family friend, now he stood tall and strong at the forefront of her and Madeline's uncertain future. She knew she could depend on him and look to him for guidance. Their recent conversation had made that abundantly clear.

But as soon as these thoughts entered her head, she shoved them aside. She had never thought of Andrew in such a way, and it frightened her. She had been in love with James; she could never acquire such feelings toward Andrew. She simply wouldn't allow it. She admitted to herself that she was grateful for Andrew's presence, but nothing more. There could never be anything but friendship between them.

The meal passed without Caitlyn saying a word. She was too lost in her whirling thoughts to interact with anyone, particularly Andrew. When the dishes had been cleared away, Andrew and her father remained at the table, lingering over their coffee and talking about the latest construction going on in town. After tidying the kitchen, Mrs. Schmidt took her mending into the parlor, and Caitlyn retrieved a bowl of peas that had yet to be shelled from beside the stove. She took her work outside where she wouldn't be required to converse with anyone. She kept her eye on Madeline as she played on the swing, and Caitlyn watched as the child successfully pushed the swing forward, now able to create her own momentum without any help. Her laughter and squeals of delight distracted Caitlyn from her troublesome thoughts, but only momentarily.

Andrew and her father must have joined her mother in the parlor, for it wasn't long before she heard the three of them talking together, their voices easily carrying to her through the open window. At first, their conversation was nothing out of the ordinary; they discussed upcoming church events, repairs being made to the schoolhouse, and the condition of the crops. Their voices droned on in the background in accompaniment to Madeline's playful antics. But when Caitlyn heard her name mentioned, she startled to attention.

Beyond the Fury

"Did Caitlyn seem a little... different to you at supper tonight?" Andrew inquired of her parents.

"She *did* seem unusually quiet," her father replied. "But then again, the storm has changed her. She isn't the same girl she was at the beginning of the summer. You're right, Andrew. Something just wasn't right with her tonight."

"I've been trying to get her to talk for days," her mother said. "She hasn't said much, other than when she talks about Madeline. She seems to think that she's assumed full responsibility for her. She rarely accepts any help... even from us."

"I think I may have something to do with that," Andrew said softly. Caitlyn strained to hear him through the partially opened window. "We talked for quite awhile about this very thing just a few days ago. I told her that she was the best person to care for Madeline. I could tell that she wanted to care for her, even though she tried to convince me that I deserved to play a bigger role in Madeline's life. I told her that I would be perfectly content carrying on as we are now, and Madeline would remain here. But she must have misunderstood. I'm not leaving her to raise Madeline on her own; but yet, I won't have the same influence on Madeline's growth as she will."

Caitlyn couldn't stand to hear him speak of her as if she weren't present. True, she was outside and he had no idea she could understand every word he said. Still, she had a right to partake in such a conversation, especially since it concerned Madeline. She rose to her feet so suddenly, peas and pods spilled from the bowl on her lap. But she disregarded the mess. She hurried into the house, heedless of the disturbance she would inflict upon their quiet conversation.

"I guess we never really came to an actual agreement," Andrew said as Caitlyn stormed into the parlor.

"No we didn't," she said with a defiant edge to her voice. "What did you *think* we agreed to, Andrew?"

Andrew had risen from his chair when she entered the room, and even though her appearance must have caught him by surprise, he walked calmly toward her. When he stood mere feet in front of her, he stopped and simply stared at her, the distance between them vibrating with tension.

"I'm sorry, Caitlyn," he said softly, his eyes filled with an intensity she had never seen before. "I only wanted you to know that I was happy with this... arrangement."

"But what *is* the arrangement?" she asked. His quiet demeanor had calmed her somewhat, and she sank into an unoccupied chair, clasping her trembling hands together in her lap.

"I'm not sure myself," he responded, looking down at her. She saw the confusion etched in his eyes, and she couldn't understand the feelings that welled up in her at that moment. "What do you want for Madeline, Cait? If you want me to go, I will. I'll visit as often as you'd like. Just tell me what you want from me."

"Don't go," she whispered, surprised that she had uttered the words. "Madeline needs you. She'd miss you terribly if you went away. I'll understand if you want to take her—"

"Caitlyn, I've already told you. I don't feel it's my place to raise her. I just can't."

"But you seem to think that I can?"

"Yes." He spoke with such confidence that Caitlyn found it difficult to avoid his gaze. Andrew extended his arms outward, encompassing both her parents as they sat silently observing the exchange. "You have your ma and pa right here to help you. And I won't desert Madeline. If you let me, I will be right there beside you, making sure Madeline is well provided for."

"You don't seem to mind that you would always be a visitor here? Madeline would never be yours."

"She never was mine," Andrew said softly. "She was Matthew and Rena's. I was just her uncle."

"And I'm her aunt," Caitlyn said in response. "But that doesn't mean you can't accept equal responsibility for her too. I'm giving you the option, Andrew, of becoming her guardian. I'm sure Matthew and Rena would approve if—"

Andrew shook his head. "There is no way we could equally take responsibility for Madeline unless... well..." His voice trailed off as he looked to her parents. "No, Caitlyn. Madeline is better off with you."

"You're sure?" Caitlyn's voice trembled as she met his eyes once more. She saw the unwavering assurance even as she spoke, and when he nodded in reply, she felt unexpected tears brimming in her eyes.

"But it isn't fair," she mumbled, mortified that she couldn't seem to banish her tears.

"Caitlyn, honey, of course it isn't fair," her mother said softly. "You both have a deep love for Madeline, and that's obvious. But Andrew is right. There is no easy way to equally see to her care, unless of course… No, you wouldn't…"

"I wouldn't what, Mama?" One glance into her mother's solemn eyes, and she immediately knew that Andrew must have had the same thought. And when she looked to him, she saw the disbelief in his piercing, blue gaze.

"Well, Caitlyn," Andrew said gently. "It seems that the only way we can solve this little dilemma of ours is t-to… to be married." He spoke so softly, Caitlyn wasn't sure she had heard him correctly. "But I'm sure your ma didn't mean to imply—"

The room blurred in front of her as Caitlyn took a few steps backward. She and Andrew married? Why, it was the craziest thing she had ever heard! What was her mother thinking? Only months ago she had planned to pledge herself to another man. She couldn't possibly marry Andrew…not now, not ever. And she said so.

"I couldn't— We couldn't—"

Her tearful interjection broke the silence that had settled over the room as she turned to the door. She fled from the parlor, sobs shaking her body. She tore down the porch steps, running, but not knowing where she was going.

"Caitlyn!"

She heard Andrew's voice behind her, but she didn't acknowledge him. She pressed onward, mindless of everything. When she tripped over the hem of her skirt and stumbled forward, she would have fallen if Andrew hadn't reached out to her. She found herself held upright by his strong arms, preventing her from tumbling into the vegetable garden.

"Are you all right?" he asked against her hair. He didn't release her, and for a moment, she relaxed against him. Her breath came in ragged gasps, but it was not due to her exertion. Tears coursed down her cheeks, but she made no move to hide them. He held her while she cried, seeming to sense that she needed this release. He said nothing while he waited for her tears to subside. When her sobs quieted, Caitlyn came back to reality so suddenly that she pushed against him until she had released herself from his embrace. To think, she had let him hold her like this! He had seen it all— the tears, the resurfacing grief. He must think her weak and helpless to react in such a way.

"I'm sure your ma didn't mean to upset you," came Andrew's soft voice. "She wasn't thinking."

"No, she wasn't," Caitlyn said with a sniffle. "I couldn't marry you, Andrew. It's only been—"

"I know," he whispered. He reached for her hand and gently cradled it in his. "Now is not the time to even consider such a thing... not after James and everything else that's happened."

Caitlyn hoped he could read the gratitude in her tear-filled eyes. This time, the tears did not exist out of grief and anger, but mere evidence of his kind consideration.

"It's not that marrying you repulses me," she said quietly. "Any girl would be blessed to have you as a husband... even me. But if we married, it wouldn't be for the expected reasons. It would have to be for Madeline."

Andrew nodded. "But what your mother suggests might not be as far-fetched as you think, Cait."

"Andrew, please. I—"

"Just hear me out, Caitlyn, please," he practically whispered, placing a hand on her shoulder. "I don't want to hurt you. But the truth is, I would love nothing more than to care for Madeline... and you, when the time is right... only when you would agree to such an arrangement."

"Arrangement?" Her voice trembled at the sudden realization. "You mean marriage?"

Andrew nodded as he drew her close. "When you're ready," he assured her. "And even then, we must do things properly. I would have to court you, formally ask for your hand... But there's time for all of that later."

Caitlyn nestled close to him, marveling at the sudden peace that stole over her. She felt so at ease and protected in his arms, and the realization startled her. Again, she felt with certainty that she could depend on him. She could trust him to hold to his word. He was offering security and a future for Madeline... even for herself. She knew she should feel overjoyed at the prospect, but the possibility was almost too great to comprehend.

Overwhelmed with it all, she met his gaze, finding his eyes brimming with tears. "You asked me what I wanted for Madeline," she whispered, resting her hand on his arm. "And it's you, Andrew. I don't want you to have to look on at a distance while I raise her. She needs you... I need you to make sure that she's happy and given everything she needs."

"Are you saying that you agree to the arrangement then?"

Caitlyn could hear the longing in his hopeful words, and she smiled up at him. "But as you said, in time. We must be sure we are doing what is best for Madeline."

He nodded. "For Madeline," he said, grasping her hand as if to make formal the commitment.

She squeezed his hand in return and smiled ever so slightly. Her agreement was spoken with renewed confidence and reassurance as she repeated, "For Madeline."

June 12, 2006

Dear Reader,

    Today marks the anniversary of the cyclone that struck New Richmond, Wisconsin on June 12, 1899. This tornado is considered to be one of the strongest recorded in Wisconsin history. With the Gollmar Brothers' Circus in town, close to 1,000 additional visitors were present in town that day. Consequently, both locals and visitors endured the storm's fury. The cyclone, which began as a waterspout over Lake St. Croix, moved on a steady, northeasterly course toward New Richmond. The storm leveled a path through the center of town, destroying homes and businesses in its wake. A 3,000-pound safe was said to be carried the distance of a full block, physically demonstrating the deadly power of the cyclone, which has since been rated F5, the highest ranking on the scale that measures a tornado's strength. Sadly, the storm claimed the lives of approximately 117 and injured around 200. But despite the loss of life and widespread destruction, residents worked to rebuild the city, and less than six months later, New Richmond had nearly 100 newly constructed buildings. The survivors looked to the future with courage, dedicated to make the town a home for their families once more.

    I received the inspiration to write this story after witnessing a tornado myself. One afternoon in June of 2005, I returned home from a day spent in Baldwin, a 20-minute drive from New Richmond, only to be alerted to a tornado skirting our property. The funnel cloud, easily visible from two miles away, severely damaged portions of nearby Hammond. Although I have always been fascinated by weather, the close encounter with the storm did not fully grab my attention until I read an article in the local newspaper. The feature told of a devastating twister that hit New Richmond 106 years previous. That's when my mother said to me, "There's your story." And as they say, the rest is history.

    Although *Beyond the Fury* is a fictional account of this event, I wanted to present a story true-to-life and realistic in nature. The characters are completely fictional, even though there is an occasional reference to a family name that originated in New Richmond at that time. I have refrained from referring to places of business by their names, hoping to obscure the identities of owners and proprietors.

Descriptions of the tornado's assault on New Richmond are based on eye-witness accounts contained in *The New Richmond Tornado of 1899: A Modern Herculaneum* and *Not to be Forgotten... 1899 Cyclone: "A Testimony of Survivors."* I am indebted to these resources as well as additional research regarding Wisconsin weather patterns, tornadoes, and the effects of such storms.

Caitlyn's encounters on Main Street following the storm are also fictionalized, although there are several references to real events with a slight twist to the actual occurrences. Such examples are the man trapped underneath the chimney and the girl holding the dead baby.

The Gollmar Brothers' Circus actually did take place on June 12, 1899, and I have taken an excerpt from a poster advertisement found in Mary A. Sather's book *They Built their City Twice: A History of New Richmond, Wisconsin.* Again, I am grateful for such detailed background on this particular time in New Richmond's history.

With this fictional account, it is my intent to portray an accurate depiction of what happened on that day, using Caitlyn's family as the center of the action. The death, injury, and destruction were very real and changed lives dramatically. But as stated earlier, the citizens of New Richmond did not allow the tornado to destroy their dedication. They reconstructed their city, and now New Richmond is a thriving community with a population of over 7,000. Just east of the Twin Cities metro area, New Richmond offers a small town atmosphere amidst the bustling cities just over the Minnesota border.

I have learned a great deal from my work on this novella, and I hope you have garnered an awareness of these events told through the eyes of fiction. It is my prayer that I have communicated truth as well as told a worthwhile story.

Thank you for reading,

Cassandra Lokker